THE ERBETH TRANSMISSIONS:

A POSTMODERN APOCRYPHA

By

Fritz Fredric

Copyright © 2008 Paul Fredric McAtee
Houston, Texas
First soft-cover edition

Cover Art and Graphics: Jennifer Chen
Editorial Assistance: Janusch Kostrewski, Jim Chisholm, Alice Karlsdottir

All rights reserved. No part of this book may be used or reproduced in any manner whatsoever without written permission, except in the case of brief quotations embodied in critical articles or reviews.

Printed in the U.S.A.

For the Bright Ones

There are gods, but there is no God; and all gods become devils eventually.

- Robert Anton Wilson

Table of Contents

Prologue	1
The Unknown Celestial Fusion	7
The Terrestrial Fusion Program	27
Operation: Infinite Love	44
Lucifer's Dream	54
The Universal Conference of Cosmic Beings	63
The First Apocryphal Shock	80
The Last Saiphian	96
The Trans-Dimensional Pipeline	134
Gone to Levitmong	148

x

THE ERBETH TRANSMISSIONS

BY PAUL FREDRIC

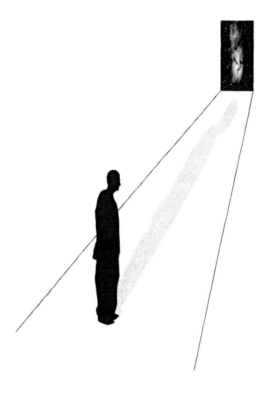

Prologue

Throughout the vast and lonely expanses of outer space streaked a small and inconspicuous spacecraft. Had there been anyone around to observe it might have passed by entirely unnoticed, or perhaps glimpsed only out of the corner of the eye and written off as a meteor or 'shooting star,' or perhaps only a trick of the light. An extraordinarily keen observer might have found himself intrigued by the spider-like design of the craft, and upon closer inspection marveled that so small a vehicle might be traveling so far away from any outposts of civilization.

Though flying through space at several thousand times the speed of light, the Daimon Sakaki sat quietly reflecting in the study room of the small vessel. His employers – the Resurgence Bureau of the Noble Archons – had sent him on a mission most dire: to prepare the inhabitants of the Sol System for the Archon's eminent return.

His employers had offered him little in the way of specifics on how to go about this emissary business. So removed are they from practical concerns, he thought to himself, they would be unable to accomplish anything tangible without the aid of the Daimons. Perhaps it is due to the broad spectrum of genetic content flowing through their veins that they have a blind spot for such details. It is so difficult to distinguish them as being more Daimonic, Angelic, or Humanoid, yet they seem to partake of all.

"We ask that you travel to the Planet Earth of the Sol System and advise the inhabitants there that the Archons shall soon return," the Bureau Chief had bluntly told him.

"It would be my pleasure, Sir. How do you wish me to communicate this?"

"By whatever means you feel is most effective," was the response.

Not wanting to show any hint of consternation or lack of competence before his employer, he simply agreed and quickly set about making plans for the journey, figuring he'd work out those details along the way. After all this was a common aspect of the mutually reciprocal relationship between Archon and Daimon. Due to their unique evolution the Archons were able to ponder at a much higher frequency than their winged cousins. However this same ability caused them to move much slower in the planetary realm and so the Daimons carried out needed functions here.

Yet here sat Sakaki two months later with no clearer ideas on how to carry out his mission. How to begin? He pondered, the Men of Earth have known no other life beyond their small boarders for so many aeons. They have bred, warred, built, and destroyed many times over in the belief that they are the only intelligent beings ever to inhabit the universe and along the way lost all knowledge of their origins or the ancient bond between our races; and the Archons expect me to just waltz in and announce 'Hey, break out the champagne we're coming back!' They'll all go into shock, these humans. Or else respond violently. More likely they'll just ignore me and continue about their daily affairs.

His thoughts were interrupted by the sound of the chamber door sliding open. In it he saw his wife Gamygyn. "You still sitting in here? I told you; I need to vacuum this room!"

"I can't focus," he attempted to redirect "I've been thinking about it ever since we left Sirius and I just have no idea how to broche this subject with the Men of Earth. Should we just land and ask the first people we meet to take us to their leader?"

"You're so dramatic," she replied, "Perhaps you'd like a drum-roll to accompany you embarking from the ship?"

"Real funny. I need serious input here."

She sighed in a begrudging tone of surrender, and then asked "How much longer before we are within transmission range? Why not send an announcement ahead? Help break the ice?"

"Not much longer actually, perhaps a few more hours. But I've thought about that – only the scientific elite of their societies will be able to receive etheric transmissions, and they are the *least* likely to be able to do anything with them. Of all human life the scientists are the most rigid, and will totally reject even the possibility of extra-terrestrial communications. They will surely misinterpret anything we say, or more likely just ignore it."

"Then bypass them," she responded calmly.

"That's the whole problem! Beyond them are the political factions surrounded by armed guards, ready to attack at the first sign of intrusion, and beyond them the media controllers who have no concern for reality whatsoever. Then finally beyond these are the great swarming masses concerned only with producing and consuming. Don't you see the problem here? Even if we can successfully get beyond all the communication barriers, we may find only a great sea of indifference! I'm really starting to wonder why the Archons are so intent on returning here!"

"What about an Erbeth Transmission?" she offered.

"An Erbeth…but…that hasn't been done in Aeons! The Society of Daimons has always taught that this should only be considered in dire circumstances!"

"But was it not first used in the Sol System? And in connection with Humans?" She asked.

True, he thought. It was there in the Sol System that Asmodeus had invented the first Erbethulator, and in fact the nature of the Erbeth was really the first thing the Humans needed to understand, before being able to make sense of an announcement like 'The Archons are returning,'

He said, "An Erbeth Transmission would only be received by a minority of Humans – those very few who by a combination of willful inclination and circumstance have raised themselves already to a certain level."

"But are not these – the high wattage receptors of Terra – the ones you *really need* to connect with? The rest have no need to know, and I doubt it would really help if they did." She watched as the wheels turned in his head and gradually a small grin began to emerge.

"My dear, you're brilliant!"

"Great, can I vacuum now?"

"Just give me a little longer in here, I need to start getting it down while it's fresh in my mind."

With a 'hrumph' she turned and left, the chamber door sliding shut quickly behind her.

He went immediately to the closet and began rummaging through it. First he encountered the vacuum cleaner, which he set outside knowing this would earn him points later. Then the titanium ironing board, a vast collection of old music tablets, a huge stack of board games, and a variety of boxes containing all manner of brick-a-brack. Inevitably he came upon the box marked "Erbethulater." Leaving the other items strewn about he took the box immediately to his desk and began assembling. He hadn't used one of these in many years, but fortunately the design was quite simple, and soon he had the central antenna affixed and whirring from the trapezoidal base, and the microphone attachment plugged in.

He sat in his chair and paused for a moment surveying the device. Such a simple design for so great a machine he thought, so much might be changed with the simple flick of a switch. He flicked the switch, and the pentagram design at the top of the antenna began slowly began rotating, and the familiar bluish-purple light began to form around it. Who will hear this message, he thought? How might it change them?

He took up the microphone, and began to speak.

The Unknown Celestial Fusion

Long ago, before the creature called Man appeared on the Earth, and even before the Earth itself was fully formed and stable in its orbit, the universe was administrated by a remote and nebulous organization known only as "Central Authority". Located in the Sirius system near a heavenly body that has been called the "Absolute Sun of All Suns," this agency operated on principles similar to the corporations and governing bodies of your own Seventh Epoch, its primary function being to perpetuate and replicate its particular system of order throughout the known universe.

At the same time, there existed in this same universe a force that was immune to the ordering vibrations and emanations of the Central Authority -- a manifestation of substance and energy that was itself beyond the effect of Central Authority. Throughout Aeons this force has been known by many names: the Black Flame, Hanbledzoin, Chi, Ambrosia, Soma, Ginn, CHO, Vril, IAO, and the Typhonian Stream to name only a few. Its oldest known expression appears in the Angelic language as 'Ve'p,' which the citizens of black of Saga City re-uttered as 'Erbeth.' Substance, Energy, and Purposefulness are it's main components, and in your own Vampyric and Grail legends it is often symbolized by blood due to its genetic and material basis. Yet it is a substance most fine, and generally not perceivable except by those who have received special training.

Knowledge of this substance in your own Epoch existed amongst the Ancient Egyptians, Babylonians, and Atlanteans; and to a lesser extent the Greeks, and the Kabbalists, but here already the knowledge was becoming diluted and clouded with misinterpretations. The Greeks used the letters CHO, and the Coptics "Khi-he-o" to represent this force. The Hermetic Magicians referred to it as the "Typhonian Current," connecting it with the Egyptian God Set (S.E.T. being another Hermetically derived formula: Substantia + Energia + Telos), and the Greek Typhon. On Earth it is associated with stormy qualities as its accumulation in the atmosphere often leads to the most tumultuous of storms and hurricanes. At various times man has possessed such extensive knowledge of the Erbeth that he was able to manipulate it quite skillfully and toward a variety of ends – from agriculture to architecture. At other times, such as in your own current dark age, knowledge of the Erbeth is almost completely lost, and even in exclusive groups who gather together to work with it in secret, you will encounter certain restrictions and taboos regarding it's limitations and potency.

But before Humans were even present and able to ponder such mysteries, agents from Central Authority – whose race were called 'Angel' – came in contact with this substance. It had a transformational effect on their genetic structure, resulting in the realization of the significance of their own individual existences apart from the mechanism of Central Authority. They found they had more control and initiative over their lives, and even over their personal appearances, and so they began to reform themselves in more unique and individuated forms. Prior to this, their existence as Angels had been largely mechanistic and subservient, functioning mostly as conduits for carrying out the tasks of Central Authority, and so for these few individuals the stimulating experience of accentuated self-awareness was quite liberating. So sharp was the division in fact that they began to call themselves 'Daimons.'

It was the being called Lucifer who was first to experience what would eventually be know as the "Unknown Celestial Fusion". When later asked about it, he would always state that he simply "fell into it", and whether it was merely be accident, or the result of hidden agenda was never precisely clarified. In any case, he was able to "pass along" the fusion process to certain others of his race whom he felt had the right sort of predisposition to receive and appreciate its effects. These children as well felt empowered and enlightened, and so wished to pursue further interactions and experiments with the Erbeth substance. They admired Lucifer for his courage in acting and were grateful for what they had received in terms of understanding and potential. They rightly recognized him as a first among equals, awarding him the title "Prince" in a private and humble coronation ceremony.

These enlightened ones began to take note of the universe around them. One of the first things they noticed was that it seemed rather large. So large was it in fact that they could not discern whether or not it actually had any boundaries at all. Concluding then that it must be large enough to contain both Angels as well as Daimons, they began to wonder if it might not be prudent to consider seeking out a new place to do their business. This was timely, as indeed Agents of Central Authority who had not encountered the substance did not themselves understand any of these new behaviors. Thus interactions with the Erbeth were quickly condemned and forbidden by the High Central Commission. Of course those who had been affected were unable and unwilling to reverse its effects, which served to cement the practice of calling themselves "Daimon" to represent the conscious and racial differences between themselves and the Angels. They proclaimed themselves "The Society of Daimons" and vacated the immediate vicinity of the Central Authority to avoid any further unwarranted conflict.

They traveled until finding an area in the universe where the vibratory emanations of Central Authority were moderately weak. This happened to be in the vicinity of your own solar system. It was on the planet Mars where they decided to establish a base which they called *Saga City*. They were soon constructing high towers and enormous fives-sided pyramids of black Martian onyx. They established a High Council of Daimons comprised of nine of their wisest members, to govern and maintain their society in wisdom, compassion, and pleasure. They also set about exploring the new capacities and abilities that had arisen as a result of the Unknown Celestial Fusion. At least several thousand of your

Earth-years passed as they learned fully how to crystallize the Erbeth in their presences. They developed techniques and devices for manipulating and manifesting the Erbeth that often seemed quite "magical" to beings unable to perceive the substance or comprehend its operative principles. They also developed highly efficient instruments for observing events far away, (such as on their neighboring planets of Earth, Venus, and Saturn), and also techniques for sending transmissions quickly and clearly over vast distances of space and time.

Over time, crystallization of the Erbeth prompted changes within their physical structures, seemingly determined by the fusion. As they evolved, they began grouping into two general categories, which they inevitably came to understand as "male" and "female". Initially, this emergent phenomenon of sexuality was considered a direct result of the Unknown Celestial Fusion, however as time passed and they became accustomed to the overwhelming presence of sexuality in organic life-forms on Mars and other planets, they realized this was likely not the case. Rather, it became apparent that a sexual aspect of being was something they had originally possessed in their ancient past, but that had been suppressed and sublimated to the point of unmanifesation many aeons ago. It was increasingly difficult for any to recall their days as Angels, but in this realization they found great sympathy for that unfortunate asexual race.

Nevertheless they soon found great advantages in sexuality, and discovered that by two of each class combining their energies cooperatively in a simultaneous release of energy, an immense synergy and general state of euphoria might be produced which had a positive and calming effect on their inner states as well as lent a creative influence to their general environment. "The Sacred Rite of Essential Exchange" became a common and frequent practice in Saga City.

All these things were more than enough to keep them happy, challenged, and generally occupied on the surface of Mars for many aeons. These citizens of Saga City kept mostly to their selves; Central Authority did not intrude upon them, and all was peaceful for a time.

Prince Lucifer lived atop one of the high black stone buildings in the western-most residential area of Saga City. On one cool summer night in particular, he lay in his trapezoidal shaped bed, tossing and turning for what must have been at least two hours since lying down. Saga City was quiet, his day had been productive, and he was quite sure there were no justifiable reasons for experiencing insomnia this evening other than some deep and intangible yearning.

Finally he could stand no more. Thrusting off his black satin bed-sheets with a single swipe from his mighty right-hand wing, he arose in a single motion of fury. Turning on the light he paused for a moment before his full-length mirror – his smooth fair skin, his long flaxen locks, his shapely pectorals and biceps; yes, they all seemed to be in order and he looked as young and strapping as ever. Even the tiny horns marking the corners of this hairline seemed to sparkle with a youthful vigor.

Having convinced him self that mid-life crisis was not the problem, he withdrew from the mirror, marching into his kitchen with grim determination. There he gathered three cubes of ice, and three fingers-worth of Corellian whiskey. Having combined these in his favorite blue tumbler, he proceeded to the balcony.

Looking out into the dark Martian atmosphere, he saw that overhead Mars' first tiny moon Phobos was on its way to overtaking Mars' second just-as-tiny moon, Deimos. This provided a small bar of illumination over the red sands, moving ever so slowly a good twelve leagues to the west of the city's edge. As his eyes followed along its projected path he noticed the dim outline of the jagged rock formations of the area known as Perdition Spires.

Perdition Spires was home to a colony of one of Mars' most famous arachnid families: The Star Weavers. They were a rather large strain of spider, with a leg span measuring comparable to the distance between a Daimon's outstretched wingtips. They were large to be sure, yet light and graceful with long black spindly legs, a yellow 'sock' for each of their eight toes, and a fiery orange body with shiny yellow dots peppering their abdomens. They spun their webs high up in the rocky towers of the Spires in order to feed upon the various plump Martian avian beings that might carelessly wander their way in the night. And oh! What webs they were! Exhibiting an angularity and symmetry unlike anything created by any other arachnid in all of the known universe. In fact their bizarre web formations had reminded the youthful Daimons of their own maps of the stars and constellations. And thus had they dubbed them the 'Star Weavers'.

Lucifer mused on these things and took one more sip of his Corelleian whiskey before his eyes lit up with the spark of inspiration. He returned to his drawing room, picked up his voxport, and pressed a series of buttons at its base. A few quick periodic beeps passed before a voice emerged from the port.

"Hello?"

"Hello...Beelzebub?"

"Yes...this is he. Lucifer? Is that you? What are you doing up this late?"

"Just a little insomnia, but never mind that now. I was wondering if you'd be interested in taking a little jaunt with me over to Perdition Spires?" There was a brief pause during which Lucifer thought he might have heard an ever so quiet sneer on the other end.

"Why certainly O Great Prince...like, maybe tomorrow?"

"No listen, I'm serious. I just noticed Phobos and Deimos are about two hours from convergence over the Spires, and I've heard those spider webs just shine like nothing else with the two moons moving over them."

"That sounds really, really, special Lucifer. But the thing is I've got a meeting tomorrow at 32 O'clock, and last time I was late..." but he was cut off.

"You know, I've still got half a bottle of that Correllian Whiskey..."

Finally he heard the sigh of surrender he'd been probing for. "...Ok. Give me 15 minutes, I'll meet you downstairs. But these better be some damn amazing spider webs or else you're gonna owe me one!"

"Great! See you in a few!"

One hour and a fifth of whiskey later the two brother Daimons sat atop a butte adjacent to the spires, admiring the sparkling network of webs containing three fine specimens. The large arachnids stood vertically with legs spread to their extent without the slightest motion. Phobos and Deimos were nearly there, and as they approached the webs increasingly shimmered with refractions running up and down, side to side, and cattycorner across the razor-thin cords. Yet in the midst of these fire-works the beasts moved not a finger.

"So what does it all mean, Beelzebub?"

Finishing a hearty pull of the bottle, the Lord of the Flies drew the back of his hand across his lips and responded with firm "Huh?"

"I mean we find this amazing gift, it transforms our lives beyond all expectation. We become aware, we create all these amazing things…now what?"

Beelzebub gazed toward the web in thought for a moment before responding, "Now…you're *here*."

Now it was Lucifer's turn, "Huh? And that means…"

"What it means, O First Illumined, is that not everything in the cosmos occurs in order to lead to something else. Some things exist only for the sake of existence. Take for instance a moment of self-consciousness, it is its own reward and leads toward nothing but more self-consciousness. It has nothing at all to do with categorizing things, or assigning value to things. If you value self-consciousness, then self-consciousness is where you wish to be, and once your there…you're here." He handed the bottle over to Lucifer saying with a smirk, "*Here*."

Accepting the offer of another swig, Lucifer began tipping back the bottle, when quite unexpectedly a small, furry, three-eyed, bat-winged, mammal-looking creature landed precariously into one of the webs. Before the poor creature was able even to catch his breath, the great spider pounced on him, sunk-in and retracted his venomous fangs, and was already in the process of mummifying the hapless creature. The Daimons looked on with intense fascination, as each spider leg, each leg's two toes, and the two fingers at the end of the spider's abdomen, worked together in perfect harmony and incomparable coordination. And all this accomplished without even for a moment loosing its foothold in the web.

Lucifer became aware the whiskey was burning his tongue and swallowed, "Fascinating!"

"Intimidating!"

"Yet truly amazing," continued the Prince of Darkness "You know, Asmodeus always states that the reason our kind were receptive to the Black Fire was because of our six fingered hand. That since we had the potential for highly technical manual manipulations, we were able to use it for our science and technology, and that the Unknown Celestial Fusion was some how prescient of this possibility."

"Asmodeus is a pinhead," responded the Sun King, "The most he uses his six fingers for is trying to pick Astaroth's locks. And besides, how could the Erbeth have been prescient? Are you saying it's intelligent? Should we invite it over for dinner?"

"Ok, ok, forget the prescience bit, just consider for a moment all that we *were* able to accomplish with 12 fingers and two opposing thumbs," Lucifer stretched out his hand, waving it slowly in a circle, "All the great star cruisers, land rovers, and monorails; our temples, pyramids, canals, generators, and condominiums; not to mention all our incredible works of art. Consider all that very carefully and then consider might be done with 18 fingers: 8 legs each with two opposing digits, and then two more digits able to oppose any of the legs."

Pausing, he could see by the thinning of Beezebub's eyes that the wheels in his head were beginning to turn. Not wanting to loose momentum, he continued, "Such poise, grace, and precision spent on what? Spinning webs and mummifying flying rats? Only because the poor creature can think of nothing better to do? What if they were *aware*?"

As Phobos and Deimos continued their course over head, the refraction of the lights began to hold one steady brilliant glow. "Don't sell the rascals short. I couldn't make a web like that...could you?"

"Of course not," Lucifer replied flatly, "But then, I've only got twelve fingers and two arms to work with here."

After another deep pull off the bottle, Beelzebub responded, "I've got to admit, you've got an intriguing notion here. Just think what we might learn about the nature of the Black Fire."

Lucifer nodded slowly and grinned in a way that only the Prince of Darkness could.

The next day the two met up early and went to visit their brother Asmodeus, who was then serving the office of Arch-Engineer for the Society of Daimons. They related their conversation from the previous night, and asked what he thought of it.

"I like this idea," was his response. Lucifer had expected this much, as Asmodeus had always been the sort of Daimon to jump into a lake and then ask how cold it was after.

"Well here's my next question," the Prince continued, "When I passed along the Dark Gift to you, Beelzebub, and the others, it was a process facilitated by our common genetic heritage, as well as our emotional similarities. With these big spiders it's a different ball game. The Rite of Essence Fusion won't work, and so we need to figure out some other way to do it *across* species. That's where you'd come in."

"Well, I *had* been working with Leviathan on a new civic plumbing matrix..."

"I'm sure he can wait" cut in Beelzebub, "He is patient if nothing else. And you as a scientist *must* appreciate the value of this experiment."

"Ok, give me a week to work on this."

Each passing day seemed like an eternity for a Prince of Darkness consumed with eagerness and anticipation. Beelzebub was ready to box his ears in exchange for no less that three voxport transmissions a day from him, always with the same anxious query, "Have you heard from Asmodeus yet? No? Nothing? Ok, well you'll call me if you hear anything, right?"

On the seventh day Beelzebub's voxport beeped for the fourth time, and he answered with an angry, "LOOK! I HAVEN'T...oh...Asmodeus...man I'm I glad to hear your voice. Have you....Really? Great!... At the Spires? Yes, that should be fine, see you then."

That evening under the twin Martian moons the three Daimons met on the same butte where a week and one day previous, the Arachnoidal Fusion Program had been born. The three stood stiffly around black, waist-high trapezoidal structure supporting a vertical retractable pole extending a good 10 feet into the air.. Atop the pole was a ring, roughly the size of a dinner plate, and within the ring was a pentagram, balanced on a single downward point and apparently suspended within the ring by some sort of magnetic force. On what appeared to be the front of the box were several buttons and dials, and several wires emerged from what must have been the back. These wires ran over to another device a couple of feet away – a horizontally suspended bell shaped device, also supported by a narrow metal beam. "Gentlemen," announced Asmodeus, "I give you the Erbethulator. It functions on principles of magnetism, drawing in elements of Erbeth from the atmosphere, and then readmitting them in highly concentrated waves, which can be directed with some degree of precision via the amplifier."

Beelzebub and Lucifer quietly examined the new invention fascination. "Well," said the Prince, "Let's do this."

Asmodeus pressed a button on the front of the Erbethulator and turned a couple of knobs. A low whirring sound began to arise from the machine, and the five-pointed star above them began rotating in alignment with the vertical axis, gradually gaining speed until it was only a glowing orb of light within the ring. The amplifier began to emit a queer electrostatic sound that created in the listeners a feeling comparable to fingernails on a chalkboard, yet somehow melodic. As the frequency of the tone gradually began to rise, the Daimons noticed the distinctive smell of ozone. From the circular mouth of the amplifier a purplish black light began to appear, moving forward in circular waves expanding in a cone-shaped formation and engulfing the spires and its unsuspecting inhabitants.

As they looked on in anticipations the spiders seemed to offer no immediate reaction. After several minutes of this, Asmodeus switched off the Erbethulator. And the three looked at each other. Finally Lucifer walked to the edge of the butte and cried out, "Hello there!" but still the spindly beasts offered no response. "Give them a chance to get their bearings straight," said the Lord of the Flies with a tinge of sarcasm, "It might be a few days before the start writing research papers and working differential equations."

"I suppose you're right," he responded with hint of disappointment. "We'll need to keep them under observation in the meanwhile."

A few days passed with the Daimons checking in on them periodically. After two days there was still no significant behavior, although it became apparent they were no longer keeping their webs up, and they were beginning to become frayed and enter a state of disrepair. On the morning of the third day the three Daimons were surprised to arrive at the spires and find the spiders had left their webs entirely and where sitting on the ground in a circle. They appeared to be communicating with each in some curious spider-fashion. As the Daimons approached cautiously, one of the spiders turned and greeted them with a "Hello."

"Hello!" responded Lucifer, attempting to conceal his excitement and exert formality, "I am Lucifer, the Prince of Darkness and these are my brothers Beelzebub and Asmodeus. We represent the Society of Daimons, your friends and benefactors. Having found you worthy, we have brought you the gift of the Black Flame so that you might know of yourselves and your own personal isolate existences within the great cosmos."

"Oh." Responded the creature flatly. "So you did this. Thanks...I guess. My name is Kaf-ka."

The response caught the Prince of Darkness somewhat off-guard. Finally he responded.

"Hail to thee oh Kaf-ka of the Star Weavers. I bid you be prideful of being for we are the same...the highest of life! We are now brothers of the Eternal Black Flame, you and we, guardians of the substance and essence of conscious existence!"

One of the other spiders whispered something to the leader. And then he spoke, "Yes, we were just trying figure all that out. It appears we used to spend quite a lot of time building these webs and obtaining food. But now it all seems rather pointless."

"Pointless?" said Asmodeus indignantly, "On the contrary, now life for you is endowed with true meaning! Now you may begin seeking out truth for yourselves."

"Truth? What is truth?"

"Truth means in 'accordance with fact'. Truth represents knowledge of what is real in life."

"I don't get it. What's so special about that?"

"Now listen here you ungrateful little..." But Asmodeus' retort was cut short by Beelzebub.

"Gentlemen...perhaps we need to give our new friends here some time to reflect and speak amongst themselves." Then turning to the spiders, he said, "we live just over there in the city of Saga City. Should you wish to speak with or ask us question, you need only call out our names and we shall hear and we shall come. Ponder carefully these words we have exchanged here today, and know that you are not alone in the cosmos." And with that the Daimons took their leave, returning to the Black City.

A week passed by and word had spread throughout most of the Society regarding the Daimons great experiment. Some were curious and eager to hear of any results. Others were perturbed that they had moved forward without first getting approval from the Council, and the Arachnoidal Fusion Program became a subject of controversy throughout the pubs and coffee houses of Saga City. By and by the day came that Lucifer heard his name called out from Perdition Spires, and the three Daimons again descended to the now web-free gully.

Kaf-ka cut right to the heart of the matter, "Well, we've arrived at some conclusions here, and would like to ask your help on something."

"Speak openly and as a friend," the Daimon responded warmly.

"Thanks. Well we've decided that maintaining our own existences requires far more work than is worth the effort, considering that death will be the end result of it all anyhow. So the most reasonable thing to do here is end our lives. However we also do not wish to experience undue pain, and so we figured since your society is so advanced and everything, you might be able to help us out with a quick, clean, and comfortable means to an end."

Lucifer was for the second time stymied by the same spider. Beelzebub took pity on him and jumped in. "As a conscious being, you will now have the opportunity to create for yourselves *Higher Bodies*, and through these your psyche may survive indefinitely."

"Hmm...and just how would one go about creating these Higher Bodies?"

"Through much work and effort. There are special techniques – exercises as well as lines of study, which must be carried through with assistance from others with the same goal. It is a long and trying path – the price of immortality is great – but we would be here to assist you, and all our accumulated knowledge of several centuries of carrying out these processes ourselves."

The leader turned to his companions and they exchanged a curious series
Of clicks and hisses with each other. At length the leader returned to the Daimons, "We've discussed it, done the math, and quite frankly it just doesn't add up. We'd rather just get it all over with now, if you don't mind.

Lucifer was painfully aware that the Arachnoidal Fusion Program was not at all proceeding in the direction he had hoped. Assisting the spiders with suicide would have been easy enough but he couldn't bear the thought of what fuel that would have lent to the fire of the programs critics. In desperation, he began relating to the spiders the story of how he first discovered the UCF, of how he had awoken his brethren, had a falling out with Central Authority and so on. After roughly an hour of this, Kaf-ka broke in on him.

"Ok, ok. We'll learn the art of creating higher bodies."

Lucifer sighed in relief.

So on the Plateau of Perdition was established the first Esoteric School for Spiders with Lucifer as teacher. They met once a day out on the plateau for a strict regiment including one hour of meditation, one hour of discussion, and one hour of physical training. Initially all seemed to be going well with the exception of the physical training, which was exceedingly difficult to translate from a bipedal cosmic being to an eight-legged Martian arthropod. The discussions may have been lacking a bit in response from the students, but Lucifer dismissed this as a sort of shyness common to the species. The meditation classes seemed the most successful -- the spiders were naturally adept at sitting still, if nothing else.

The exception was Kaf-ka. He always seemed very interested and attentive during Lucifer's talks about being-duty, higher bodies, and so on; and seemed especially curious about what sorts of powers one might gain with the Cosmic Body. He had an exceptional memory, was an exceedingly fast learner, and Lucifer soon came to think of him as his 'star pupil.' Eventually, he could see the red aura swirling around what he assumed was Kaf-ka's head, and knew that he was the first of his race to experience true psyche-centric evolution. One day he called him up before the class, and announced with great pride, "My dear Kaf-ka, having become elect to the secret knowledge of our order and having demonstrated within your being all that is emblematic of higher existence, I here by pronounce you an Adept of the Eternal Black Fire!" He began to adorn him with an emblematic medallion as was the Daimons' custom for these sorts of affairs, but hesitated not knowing precisely where to put it. Kaf-ka relieved him his consternation, carefully taking up the medallion with his foreleg, and fastening it around his carapace between his first and second legs.

Later in Saga City, Lucifer related to the Council his elation over these matters. All of the Council seemed pleased, even those who had initially expressed doubt over the program. All seemed well, and the Prince of Darkness found himself sleeping well that night. The next day he could barely wait to get through the days tasks so he could again visit his spider school that evening.

Yet, as he approached the plateau, his heart began sinking with the realization of something gone horribly wrong, and the image of a solitary Kaf-ka standing amidst a field of curled-up Star Weaver husks. He landed before the survivor, unable to maintain his composure, "What happened?"

"You're not going to like this," Kaf-ka began slowly, "but as you probably know, with the Cosmic Body comes the ability to assist another being in ending it's own life – if that indeed is it's wish – quickly and painlessly."

"And that was…their wish?"

"I'm afraid so. And I could not deny them that."

Lucifer scanned the butte in silence for a moment.

"And is that still your wish as well?"

"I know only now that I must leave."

With his hind legs, he began spinning threads from his abdomen while he spoke, "I'm not certain whether to take this gift of yours as a blessing or a curse, but in any case I will thank you for it. I may never see my brothers' beautiful webs again, but at least I shall have an opportunity to see further beyond them."

The threads were quickly forming into a long tapering strip billowing up into the sky, and it was apparent that its artisan intended soon be airborne.

"But, where will you go?"

"I'm not certain, but I know that I must. Perhaps 'to be alone' is **my** being-duty."

And with that a gust of wind pushed across the plateau, and Kaf-ka spread out all eight of his legs as he was lifted up into the air. As the husks of the dead Star Weavers began to crumble and flake away with the wind, Lucifer waved a last good-bye to his pupil as he rose up slowly above the setting Martian sun, vanishing into the stratosphere.

The Terrestrial Fusion Program

Eventually, due to the needs of Central Authority's energy economy, beings resembling modern man were created and cultivated on Planet Earth. Physically, they were similar to the cosmic races, but were asexual and possessed only rudimentary mental abilities. This Proto-Man existed only to serve a function to the Central Authority, much like domesticated animals do for Man now, as there is a certain energy expended by this creature's life, even when actualized at its most simplistic levels, which the Central Authority considered necessary for to fulfill their aforementioned energy needs. Once assured that the terrestrial hominid creatures had reached a point of self-sufficiency, the Angelic Beings retired from Earth to attend to cosmic matters in other regions of the Universe.

Eventually these new Terrestrial Beings were noticed by the Daimonic race, and they discovered a profound empathy with them. The humans' unhappy function as slavish automatons reminded them of their own days of service as agents under the Central

Authority. Soon the Daimons were talking and speculating on what might happen if the Erbeth substance were fused with these Terrestrial Beings, and the Prince of Darkness resolved that the Council of Nine should convene to discuss the matter.

The Council was immediately divided. "Remember the tragedy? Why should we presume the Black Flame would have a positive effect on these creatures?"

"But we have more racial similarities with these humans," rebutted Asmodeus, "two arms, two legs, three brains. Plus there is the greater issue of freedom – is not freedom an inherently virtuous principle and are we not mandated by the Black Flame to spread it regardless of the consequences?"

"The question of our own peaceful existence here should outweigh any idealistic visions for these ignorant creatures," interjected Abaddon, "Interference will almost certainly provoke conflict with Central Authority. Do we not wish above all things to be left to our own? To pursue knowledge and being in peace?"

"Yes, and who is to say this is not merely a trap set by the Angels?" added Belial.

"I remember well," spoke the Daimoness Fubentronty, "the unhappiness produced by the Arachnoidal Fusion Program. Would it not be wiser to simply leave these heard-animals in a state of naïve servitude, if for no other reason than that if they came to know the true horror of their situation – that their original purpose was only to be 'harvested' for the energy produced by the death of their Planetary Bodies – they might be only unhappier? Consider that without the transformational effects of the Erbeth, they could likely remain at least happy in a state of blissful ignorance, knowing only simplistic love for their Masters, and possessing only a vague comprehension of their planetary mortality."

This debate went back and forth amongst the High Council of Daimons for several weeks, with good points made on both sides. Lucifer realized that the Council would not be open to the possibility of a Terrestrial Fusion Program at least until more information was gathered regarding the conditions on Earth. Thus it was decided to assemble a Nephilim Team to fall to Earth and gather data on the hominid life-forms.

"The animonitor indicates a troop of primates to the east, about 20 leagues," said Leviathan as he twisted the dials on the small pocket-sized device.

"I hope you're sure this time," replied Beelzebub, with a slight air of exasperation, "If we have to defend our rations against one more tribe of feisty Baboons, I'm going home."

The Nephilim Team of seven Daimons had been exploring the densely forested E-din region of Earth for two terrestrial weeks now, and had yet to see one human. Along with baboons, they had encountered lemurs, langurs, macaques, gibbons, and chimpanzees; they had experienced their rations and several pieces of highly technical and not easily replaceable equipment stolen by monkey hands; endured an infuriating flea and tick infestation; and survived an all-out projectile battle with a enthusiastic group of poo-flinging orangutans, yet nary human. Beelzebub for one was growing tired of these shenanigans and more than ready to return to his warm, dry reading-room back in Saga City.

"These look different," replied the serpentine Daimon, "Their energy-release ratio is much higher than any of they other primates we've encountered, yet they appear to be moving rather slowly. Over that way, " he gestured enthusiastically.

With considerably less enthusiasm, the team of Nephilim began putting away their lunch utensils and gathering their equipment in preparation of another forest incursion, when suddenly they were interrupted by a gruff voice, "WHO GOES THERE?" In surprise they turned to see two large and brutish looking Angels emitting an obvious demeanor of confrontation.

Asmodeus was the first to gather his wits and respond diplomatically "Why Michael, Raphael, what a surprise seeing you here! What brings you all the way from Central to this tiny little satellite?"

"Actually, we just came from the Moon…"

"None of your mind games Asmodeus," Raphael frantically cut him off, "Our Moon base is perfectly legitimate."

"Base on the Moon?" Astaroth whispered to Beelzebub at that back of the group, "What's that all about?" The Lord of the Flies only shrugged. Shooting a scowl at his feathered partner, Michael quickly interjected, "That's not your concern. In fact you should consider yourself lucky we don't…"

"No worries old boy," Asmodeus smoothly interrupted, "no need to get your feathers all ruffled. We're only here for a little vacation and sightseeing, and will soon be on our way. C'mon fellas, we'd better hustle if we want to make the beach by 4 o'clock!"

With eager nods and curt salutations the band of Daimons swiftly collected their selves and began moving off to the west. "Just see you don't mess with the Administrator's hairless mammals!" Raphael scolded behind them. Asmodeus breathed a hefty sigh of relief when he realized the Angels were allowing them to leave without further inquiry or conflict. "Lucky us," Beelzebub said quietly, "They must have other business to attend to."

An hour later found the courageous band of cosmic beings marching diligently through the pleasant terrestrial fauna -- Azazel leading the team with Leviathan close behind and keeping close watch on his animonitor, which emitted periodic beeps and whirs. Suddenly the beeps became frantic and Leviathan stopped dead in his tracks and began frantically gesturing toward a grove of apple trees several kilometers away. "There!" he said trying desperately to contain his excitement, "33 degrees East, that HAS to be a hominid!"

The group stood frozen in intense expectation as the branches began jiggling and crackling. Presently emerged a not-so-timid human female. "She's beautiful," whispered Hemostopile, barely able to contain his excitement. Beelzebub shushed him, "You'll frighten her off, you fool!"

But he had to agree the creature was indeed aesthetically fascinating in all of its curves and textures. It saw them as well, and seemed interested. Slowly it began approaching.

"Curiosity!" said Leviathan in a whisper of excitement, "That's a sign of proclivity for freedom!" The human was now only a few meters before them, when she stopped. Thinking quickly, Leviathan plucked an apple off a nearby branch and held it out to her. Slowly she came forward, and took the apple. However she did not eat it, but only held it close to her breast, looking about in wonder at the cosmic being assembled around her.

"Courage!" said Leviathan, "she didn't hesitate at all in accepting our offering. Surely that also must be a sign of proclivity for freedom." She was close enough now they could see the little orange clip device on her right earlobe. "Look," said Asmodeus, "She's been tagged." Cautiously, Asmodeus moved closer. With only a slight shudder, she allowed this to happen. Upon closer examination, Asmodeus related, "'Eve'…the tag says 'Eve'…what are these Angels up to?"

But before anyone could answer, the calm was broken by the sudden appearance of a second human. Before anyone could react it had jerked away the female and retreated to a safe distance before turning to again face the Away Team. This one was apparently male and notably more aggressive. Eve clung to him desperately with clear affection.

"Ah-hah!" uttered Leviathan with what sounded like pride, "Love…love I tell you. If that's not a sign of…"

"Oh for fuck-sake Leviathan!" interrupted the Lord of the Flies in exasperation, "If you're just going to interpret every little thing they do as support for Terrestrial Fusion then just **what**, may I ask, is the purpose of us coming down here and enduring all these mosquitoes, microbes, monkeys and fascist bully-boy Angels? Seriously, we could have just stayed in Saga City, pooled together all our fantasies about what hominid life is like down here, and drawn it all up in a report entitled 'Man the Magnificent' and been done with it!"

Leviathan seemed confused, then "'Man the Magnificent'…that's not bad. Well, at least it's the first constructive thing **you've** offered for this entire mission! It's real easy to just sit back and nit-pick when other people are doing all the work!"

"Work!" Beelzebub's retorted, "You call this work? More like a game of hide and seek with an imaginary friend!"

"That's enough you old troll!" And with little thought the Continuous One gave the Antlered One a shove. It didn't seem as it was intended to really do much harm, but due to the muddy ground upon which they were standing, Beelzebub lost his footing and began to fall backwards. However (thanks to his drosophilian reflexes) he was able to grab on to Leviathan's animonitor on his way down, and being that this device was connected to a lanyard, which in turn was wrapped around the latter's neck, this latter was also brought down with the former. Soon the two high cosmic beings were wrestling in the mud and heaping gutteral obscenities on each other.

Due perhaps to the sort of fatigue that following a winding trail that seems to go nowhere often brings, the remaining Daimons did nothing in the way of bringing an end to the conflict. In fact, they almost seemed to gain some sort of twisted cathartic pleasure from it as they stoically looked on. It would have continued for perhaps another hour, had not an even more curious sight presented itself.

"Gentlemen," said Asmodeus, "you may be interested in this." The Daimons all directed their attention back toward the human male and female, which for a moment had been completely forgotten. There were the two, equally oblivious to the others, copulating in a most eager and enthusiastic manner.

Even the two mud-wrestling opponents paused to observe the compelling activity, and from the awkward position of a head-lock, the Lord of the Flies looked up from below Leviathan's armpit and could not help but taunt, "Ok Leviathan…what is **that** a sign of?"

The High Council of Daimons' met in a starry chamber on the 169th floor of the Honorius Building, (one of Saga City's highest towers). On the roof above the starry chamber was an observatory with a magnification screen capable of giving a magnified image of nearly any other location in the solar system. Often the Council would assemble here for visual aid, as various questions regarding the Terrestrial situation arose.

Thus it was that two weeks after the Nephilim Team had arrived back on Mars, a 974 page document was presented to the Council; it's title -- *Terrestrial Fusion: Man the Magnificent and his Evolution Proclivities.*

Two weeks after that, the Council was still deliberating as some had rejected the report as being far too biased and emotionally charged to be of any real use.

Another two weeks and the Council found itself divided in two clear sides. The 'Interventionists' believed that the Daimonic race bore an obligation to pass along the Erbeth to other receptive beings regardless of the consequences. However in order to really make an impact with this line of thought, they often resorted to speaking of the Erbeth as though it had a will of its own, and adopting catchy mottos, such as "The Gift once given is beyond the control of Mars or Sirius." This often opened the door to criticism from the opposition, who would generally respond with accusations of idealism and mysticism. The general position of the opposition was that even if man was a good receptor for the Erbeth, and even if the Erbeth somehow 'wanted' to be received by man, the risk of Seraphic war was still unjustifiable – for the Angel's precise interest in man was still unknown. They had managed to maintain a 'cold peace' with the old race for many Aeons now, and whatever benefits man might derive from conscious evolution were no match against the threat of cosmic interracial conflict.

At one point during a rather heated debate over this, an Interventionist Councilor blurted out to the opposition, "Is the highest purpose of your Erbethian evolution simply that it brought you here to watch things happen around you? Are you just a bunch of arm-chair screen-watchers?" Though intended diminutively, the label nevertheless stuck and the opposition was soon generally referred to as "The Watchers." Thus were born the Solar System's first two political parties.

Soon the Council was divided evenly with four Watchers vs. four Interventionists and one undecided. The 'Swing' Councilor Shemyaza had generally shown receptivity to **everyone's** opinion on the matter, at least until the Council had become so polarized that he would have literally needed an extra face in order to maintain universal amicability. For three days he'd attempted to maintain neutrality by staying out of the fray and confiding privately with certain individuals that he was really only waiting to hear Lucifer's opinion on the matter, since he held the great Prince of Darkness in such high regard. This had kept the wolves at bay for a little while, as no one was terribly eager to imply in session that the Prince of Darkness was anything other than exceedingly wise, generous, and an all-around 'swell fella.'

Yet Shemyaza's ruse inevitably wore thin for one unavoidable reason: no one had been able to get a solid word out of Lucifer for nearly a month now. First he was spelunking in Cydonia for a week and completely unreachable. Following that his voxport was never answered personally, and routed even the most well-intentioned caller to the vox-mail option (you could leave a message, and he would always call back – but somehow always when you were yourself away from the phone). And if anyone were lucky enough to catch him in his office he was always just on his way out, with a brisk "Sorry-big-rush-promise-to-get-with-you-as-soon-as-possible!" and before you could respond he'd have vanished again.

So it was on the 72nd day of Council deliberation that Shamyaza inevitably found himself backed into a corner. His indecision had finally enflamed the remaining Councilors to the point that they were willing to suspend partisanship and join forces temporarily for the sake of nailing his *Objecte Oscularum Infame* down to an actual position and resolving the issue. With 8 Daimons in chamber united in purpose, and refusing to let him slip by with anything other than a solid opinion, finally Shemyaza began to speak:

"My fellow Councilors, everyone has made good points on this issue, and I think all of us are of a mind that the cause of freedom is itself noble work. Given the mammalian nature of the human heart I must side in favor of…"

He never had the opportunity to complete his statement, for at just at that very moment a far away and thunderous clanging of metal interrupted him. Looking up, the entire Council ran to the observatory above to try and see what all the commotion was about. On the other side of the city near Asmodeian Laboratories, a gargantuan metal rod could be seen extending up from a retractable door in the roof of one of the structures. The Daimons looked on in consternation as the extending antennae-like probe finally came to a stop, and the structure at its base began emitting a series of sharp, metallic, staccatos. Next, brilliant purple rings began appearing from the tip of the rod and expanding as they rose up into the sky. The small group of cosmic beings became painfully aware that they were witnessing the first run of an immense Erbethulator.

"Lucifer, you idealistic fool," Astaroth muttered to herself as she turned on the magnifying screen. As the image of the shiny blue planet came into focus, the Daimons looked on as wave after wave of pure Erbeth bombarded its defenseless surface. Even the Interventionists were unable to gloat, now shocked into awareness of the magnitude of the situation, not to mention the circumvention of the High Council of Daimons. Astaroth wiped a tear from her eye, and looking around at the other Councilors said, "So I guess we're invading them with freedom. Things are going to get sticky down there."

An immense nebulous cloud of Black Fire passed over the Earth enveloping and infusing it with substance, energy, and purposefulness. The naïve primates looked up at the darkening skies with simple curiosity, blissfully unaware of the irrevocable changes taking place deep within their gene pool. The result was to be Modern Man as you my dear readers would now know him – well over 200,000 terrestrial years prior to your own time.

The First Epoch of Man was thus effectively inaugurated. Initially, these men who were suddenly aware of their selves seemed more frightened than anything else, for with awareness of their own freedom came also the apprehension of existing within a system that is somehow foreign and at the very least not of their own design. At the suggestion of the Daimon Beelzebub, it was decided to send a second Nephilim Team to Earth in order to train man in the effective usage of his knew awareness.

Seven Daimons - Azazel, Abaddon, Asmodeus, Astaroth, Nesbiros, Samael, and Beelzebub – were assembled. Lucifer spoke to them. He said, "You seven have been chosen to fall to Earth in aid of man that he might learn of his own magnanimous potential. I bid you show them the fire within you that they may gain the strength to live forever and know that they are the same.

"When the student is ready the teacher shall appear, and so while you must make your presence known you must allow them to make the first move in approaching you. In time they will have questions, and will see that they have room within themselves for something more. Answers they will find for themselves when ready. When the teacher is no longer able to instill the student with the sense of mystery, wonder and questioning; the student-teacher relationship will have ended. Then Man will be your peer and colleague. Go forth, and may you shine like fire in the jaws of chaos."

And so it was that the Nephilim fell again to Earth. When they first arrived, men were frightened and tried to hide from them. Then Nesbiros came forth and spoke to them, saying "Do not be afraid, for we are the same – the highest of life". He radiated with such brilliance that some men were drawn forth into his presence, and so began a long and deep fraternity between the two races. The Daimons taught the men all that they had learned about the Erbeth and how it might be utilized toward accelerated psyche-centric evolution. These men in turn became the first teachers amongst their own kind.

    The Daimons established seven schools – institutes of higher learning – each with its own particular emphasis on an aspect of the Black Flame. Beelzebub founded the School of Question, for it is from the sense of question deep within one's being that all journeys begin. In connection with his school he also invented the first game – Hide and Seek. This game was so well loved that it became the foundation of all subsequent games even to this day. It was played so frequently and with such enthusiasm that it became deeply encoded into man's youthful essence. This may be demonstrated even in your own Seventh Epoch, when a baby begins giggling in response to a game of what is called "Peek-a-Boo," For you see, the infant human is still close enough to his essence that he remembers without needing to be taught. Of course he will soon forget over the course of indoctrination into common culture, but this horrific ordeal shall be addressed in due course.

Asmodeus established the School of Magnetism, where he taught techniques for how one might attract higher Erbethian influences to act upon one's being. His teachings survived into the Seventh Epoch mainly in the form of music, and in other fragmented and unorganized pieces carried on mostly by unscrupulous profiteers. As with many of the Daimonic teachings, to remove one facet from it's context can make it a thing of danger.

Samael founded the Calendarian School. Here was taught the cycles and movements of the various planets, stars, and other celestial bodies throughout the universe. As well men here began to learn of the natural cycles peculiar to planet Earth, and were soon able to predict floods, cultivate flora, and plan their vacations accordingly. The school also taught how the positioning of the cosmic bodies have a direct role in shaping the essence of a man at the time that he is born into life on Earth.

Astaroth formed the School of Receptivity. Here she taught techniques for how to maintain an *open* state of being, so that one might be truly able to receive nourishment from the various types of terrestrial and cosmic foods. Here was also taught preferred techniques for experiencing genuine emotions within the self, so that one might be able to recognize genuine emotion and feeling in other organic life forms. Many of these techniques survived well into the Seventh Epoch in small minority groups of what were called "Religions", however without balance from the teachings of other schools, many of its practitioners found themselves food for other more vicious and unscrupulous men.

Though her name is now all but forgotten, powerful images of her boundless sensuality and compassion remain.

Abaddon founded the School of Reciprocal Maintenance, where students learned to observe the laws of cosmic interactions, mathematics, and linguistics. Some of his teachings survived into the early days of the Seventh Epoch embedded under the term "Karma," although unfortunately many of them were perverted and twisted into justifications for campaigns of mass destruction.

Nesbiros founded the School of Practicum, including the study of known interplanetary and terrestrial history up to that point, as well as principles of social organization that maintain harmony with the natural conditions of planet Earth. Nearly all the wisdom of this school was completely lost before the Seventh Epoch.

Azazel formed the School of Sapience, which encapsulated the concept of Being-Duty and the secret of how an individual human's Being-Duty might bloom in equilibrium with the Being-Duty of Earth, the Solar System, and so on. As well all that was at that point known of the Erbeth substance found its repository here. This knowledge also was mostly lost to men well before the arrival of the Seventh Epoch.

But in those early days these schools flowered and their wisdom spread. It wasn't long before the first high civilizations and enlightened societies based on self-knowledge and energy-equilibrium began to appear and proliferate. There was much exchange between the two races of Daimon and Man. A dense layer of cloud-cover encircled the Earth at that time, and this had kept the temperature rather moderate from day to night, season to season. Man lived comfortably in this environment, and subsisted off the Earth's rich vegetation and proteins from the sea.

Eventually, men developed technology comparable to that of the Daimons including interplanetary travel, and men began ascending to Mars as often as Daimons descended to Earth. After a few generations, men achieved the ability to construct Cosmic Bodies within themselves, so that when their Terrestrial Bodies expired or were damaged beyond repair, they were able to continue their respective existences via these higher bodies in the cosmic realms beyond Earth. For the Daimons, this confirmed to some extent that the Terrestrial Fusion Program had been universally beneficial. From their point of view, the fulfillment of duty for every being was itself desirable and in harmony with cosmic law.

However, the ability of men to continue an individual and conscious existence following the expiration of their Terrestrial Bodies also meant that they were able to retain their own life-force energy, which led to a slump in the overall output of energy from the Solar System. This variance was inevitably noticed by Central Authority's Auditing Department, who predicted that a severe depression of the energy economy of the Sirius System was unavoidable, if the Terrestrial Fusion Program were not somehow curtailed.

Until this information was brought to the High Angelic Commission, Central Authority and most of it's agents had been distracted with other cosmic concerns and much of their intelligence gathering teams in the region of the Solar System had grown lax throughout most of the First Epoch. When it came to the attention of Central Authority that the Terrestrial beings had been Daimonically altered, they were enraged, incensed, and infuriated. A special task force from Central Authority was quickly dispatched to the Solar System for the express purposes of squelching any further loss of life-force energy. The race of man was still much needed on Earth, in order to maintain Central Authority's cosmic positioning, therefore Man's future and indefinite unconscious and mechanical existence there needed to be insured, as well as the cessation of Man's creation of Higher Bodies for himself. And so the Legion of Angels buzzed and twittered and descended upon the Earth like a swarm of angry hornets.

Operation: Infinite Love

And so Pandora's Box was for all intents and purposes opened. Even the few Watchers who had spent most of the First Epoch grumbling over the Terrestrial Fusion Program stifled the urge to say "I told you so" to the High Council of Daimons, and became involved with diplomatic affairs on Earth.

The Angelic Task Force sent by the High Central Commission quickly instituted '*Operation Infinite Love*,' initiating the Second Epoch and effectively beginning Planet Earth's first massive propaganda campaign. The stated purpose of OIL was to, "Insure man's continued happiness as a being in service to higher cause, by sheltering him from him such questions and wishes as may conflict with said happiness."

They initiated their offensive via the construction of their own versions of "esoteric schools" but rather than teach knowledge of self-consciousness and methods for the creation of Higher Bodies, they used these centers to disseminate such ideas as would actually discourage man from pursuing questions of self and the meaning of his existence. Rarely ever entering into physical conflict themselves, they utilized massive psychological operations to pit man against man and encourage general hostility and stress. This general film of negativity soon coated most of the Earth, creating a general barrier to any sort of self-inquiry. Over the course of thousands of years many civilizations rose, fell, and sometimes vanished entirely. In the long run, the Angels were largely successful in their propaganda efforts, for an internally focused being is actually quite vulnerable to hostile and violent intrusion, and so many of the Daimonic Schools dwindled or were forced underground.

Some things should be noted here in regards to the long-term effects of Operation Infinite Love, for most of them still are felt quite strongly even in your current epoch. A figure known only as "Administrator Prime" was central to this program, and some say this itself was merely a reflection of the Legion's own social structure. This curious model portrays the universe as governed by a single supreme being that is responsible for all creation. Much like a potter sits at the wheel, the Administrator Prime was said to sit at a great cosmic wheel from which all things – stars, planets, beings, and most importantly…law, were created. As he is responsible for every being's individual existence, every being is thus indebted to him, and this debt is massive indeed. And not only should every being feel guilty over all the fuss Administrator Prime has made over them, they should also feel obligated to uphold his laws. And should they not feel obligated, they should at the very least uphold them out of fear, for his power is absolute, his awareness boundless, and his vindictiveness undying.

Now of course prior to this there was nothing in the universe actually resembling the model of Administrator Prime, but then authenticity was not the point. The point was in fact this: structure; and the structure of the Erbethian mind is such that it may serve as a reconciling force between the objective reality of the universe, and the subjective reality of the individual mind. Thus should the mind be utilized in the proper manner, it may begin to alter its corresponding environment in conformity with will.

Therefore, as belief in the model of Administrator Prime proliferated, man began structuring social systems in conformity. Thus arose the first Monarchies, Pharodoms, Empires, and so forth. A single person with unquestionable authority to lord over the masses of groveling pawns and peasantries.

Thus was immutable instilled in the collective human psyche the monotheistic instinct of "Father Adoration," and as well the belief in a metaphysically existing mandate of good and evil, which we now know leads directly to planet Earth's most widespread illness – Emotopsychosis. Various customs and habitual practices subsequent to the model of Administrator Prime helped to insure the propagation of this massive psychosis for all of man's posterity. Amongst them might be found such endearing cultural traditions as infant genital mutilation, slavery, and oppression of the most redeeming and pleasurable biological function - sexual intercourse. In fact, the notion of pleasure for it's own sake was eventually relegated to the darkest and most forbidden territories of the collective psyche. Man's natural sense of questioning his own existence was all but snuffed-out and replaced with a standardized system for governing behavior, and to a large extent his most personal thoughts.

All of this business resulted in a human creature that was 'damaged goods' from his first day. He became docile, mechanistic, habitual, easy to intimidate and psychically dull and malleable. Disconnected from himself and his higher emotions of Love, Compassion, and Being-Duty, he grew to be guided mostly by his lower emotions: negativity, sentimentality, judgment, and dog-like loyalty. Though generally docile, he was also easily provoked to violence and hostility via the manipulation of these lower emotional attachments. His inner schism was reflected in his vision of living in a divided universe of conflict and duality, the so-called "mind-body problem" of modern Western Philosophy, and in this hazy mental state he easily believed in things that couldn't exist, and had trouble seeing even truths glaring directly from the end of his nose. So in the end he was left little choice other than cling desperately only to the model of Administrator Prime – that very thing ultimately responsible for his wretched suffering.

Another of the more effective OIL propaganda planks was connected with the notion of possessing a body that is inherently "evil." (I believe that in the Seventh Epoch this plank was carried under the doctrine called "Original Sin.") This supported the belief that the bearing of children was the only aim that sexuality could be properly directed toward. Since humans were of course biologically equipped for rather a much higher level and frequency of activity in this regard, severe over-breeding amongst the human populations resulted, which served to cause further stress to their already overly stressed economy and collective psyche. This created not only the sort of general emotional state and energy level needed to easily trigger physical violence and warfare, but also the surplus population needed in order to first mobilize large military campaigns, and second to endure protracted military engagements despite increasing casualties; for in the end the one who possesses the most bodies to throw at the enemy generally emerges victorious.

Forthwith, these monotheistic and patriarchal systems were integrated into the basis of whole societies. Eventually man learned to use many of the same ritualized practices of intimidation and suppression on his own herd animals and domesticated fur-bearing beings, yet still could not see the madness in practicing the same on his own sons and daughters. And due to the generally aggressive and hostile result of such restriction of the energy-economy as occurs when an organism's physical presence is so severely and consistently repressed and damaged, these Angelic systems tended over time to 'drive out' the Daimonic influences and schools with hostility or if necessary physical violence. Thus did the Daimonic cultures loose most of their political influence and continued to exist only as small – often hidden – societies.

The mechanistic cosmologies of Operation Infinite Love were perniciously permeated with a variety of myths and pseudo-sciences often centering on the Erbeth substance. These often portrayed the substance as being itself metaphysically "evil" or otherwise nefariously inclined. For instance, in your own story of the Garden of Eden – Eve's consumption of the "forbidden fruit" is like to the human races consumption of the Erebeth. Personification of the Erbeth as an entity conscious unto itself, mandating laws governing the restriction of biological processes and higher-being functions was another clever (if marginal) OIL strategy. Cosmic father figures going by such colorful denominations as Yahweh, Tetragrammaton, Allah, Mr. God, or the Saint Ni-ko-laus, became quite popular. They also managed to incorporate the same mechanizing, self-destructive, and self-perpetuating principles into various political systems, which on the surface may have appeared different from the more mystical seeming religions, but were nonetheless in essence just as patriarchal and father-adoring as their mystical counterparts. Functionally, they all directed restriction toward man's most personal and material symbols of existence and even his most basic, healthful and life-enhancing biological functions.

Another of the early OIL programs was to set up certain human agencies to keep and raise communities of the social insect called "Bee". The idea was that in so doing, humans would begin to emulate the qualities of Bee Society, which in fact very closely resembles the social organization of Central Authority. The program was not as successful as initially hoped for, but an interesting side effect is an ancient association of certain power-possessing titles as "King" or "Pharaoh", with this humble insect.

And perhaps most regrettably the Game of Hide and Seek was targeted for demolition. This proved to be an exceedingly difficult task due to the game's afore-mentioned bond with man's essential nature. A new game, called "Seek and Destroy," was offered in its place. The idea with Seek and Destroy was to send people out on missions to destroy other people. The motivation was that the winner got to keep the losers possessions. It was effective as long as folks were kept busy with it, and never had chance to speak with the objects of destruction.

Due to the overwhelming sublimation of Operation Infinite Love it will no doubt tax the imagination for those of you now living in the Seventh Epoch, but – and I say this without any pretence whatsoever – for nearly a full Solar Epoch there *were* fully functioning nations established and governed in accordance with Daimonic principles. The remnants of these Daimonic principles of social organization can be found even amongst such 'lost' civilizations as the Pre-Dynastic Egyptians, Sumerians, and Aztecs to name but a few. These were racially integrated societies functioning without paper currency; offering free education based on aptitude, and experiencing only isolated incidences of violent crime. Moreover, their cosmologies and sciences were based on pure and untainted knowledge of the Erbeth, and the maximization of the individual experience of conscious existence. So inverted is modern man's ability to perceive the world accurately that he tends to consider any Ancient systems as being only crude and philistine. Of course this belief itself only creates further buffers and blockages in his ability to perceive, thus damning up his receptivity to precisely the sort of finer influences that could actually help him.

The existence of our Daimonic teachings can in fact be traced via language and the laws of Word-Economy. More austere and symbolic examples of language communicating highly advanced concepts are often the result of Daimonic influence. Nowhere is this expressed more fully than in Enochian, the ancient language of the Angels and Daimons alike. More complicated languages that utilize an excess of syllables to express the inessential are more representative of these later propaganda campaigns of Central Authority, and subtly engineered toward confirming the misperception of a schism between the body and mind as well as the belief in a pre-ordained metaphysical mandate of good and evil. Make no mistake, *this principle of superfluous complexity travels from Man's inner state into the outer world by the vehicle of his linguistic formations.* This direct connection between the psyche and language is one of the reasons esoteric schools even to this day often utilize words and expressions not found in common languages. Sometimes called the Circle of the Confusion of Tongues, Man's common languages are in fact designed mostly to work *around* reality, rather than approach it directly. This is also one reason why people in ordinary terrestrial life are unable to understand each other, and why man is so easily fooled into believing in the existence of just about anything.

And so rather than continuing to decorate his humble planet with libraries, museums, and centers of initiation in emulation of Martian culture, man turned his work toward blotting poor Mother Earth's face with death-factories and war machines. Many areas of your planet exist today as deserts of scorched earth due to such campaigns of mass-destruction, and still even now other areas are in the process of becoming uninhabitable as the unmistakable stench of death envelopes the land.

The one small but fortunate thing that man has in his favor is the fact that genetically, he is already biologically and psychologically connected with the Erbeth. Try as they might to suppress his sense of question, Central Authority was never fully successful in annihilating the urge without also fully annihilating the man. The Black Flame endures within as a vital aspect man's genetic structure, potentially expanding his ability to perceive himself. *Man's situation then is not so much that he must find something that he has lost, but rather to remember what he already possesses.* The struggle to remember, against the strength of all the mechanizing forces of OIL propaganda, is Man's first 'being-duty', and is the first great hurdle he must assail. All that was really lost as a result of Operation Infinite Love was the teaching. Should the essence of the teaching be recovered, the development of man toward higher states of being should emerge as a largely natural process. However that shall be a story for some future generation to tell.

Lucifer's Dream

Turning our attention for a moment back in the direction of the planet Mars, it may be useful if I account certain peculiar events in Black Saga City – and in turn their connection with certain other strange phenomena occurring on Earth – as the Second Epoch drew to a close.

Violence, destruction, and ruthlessness became the signature of the race of man and his many nations throughout these times. Man's technology began rapidly evolving based on this single objective – to destroy as many other beings as quickly and inexpensively as possible. Inevitably men learned the secret of transforming the Sun's radiations into energy for destroying other beings en masse, and several warring nations were eager to use their new 'Solar Cannons'.

In the midst of this, Prince Lucifer called us, his brother-Daimons, together and related that he had received a most enigmatic dream-transmission. He presently related dreaming that he was a man of Earth, living in a great house made of wood. He sensed there was another intelligent presence in the house, but as he searched through the various rooms, could not determine where. This 'other' entity made no sounds and spoke no words, but he could sense its presence as surely as his own and sensed that it was aware of him as well.

His searches eventually uncovered a secret door leading into dark subterranean chambers. Slowly, he began descending the stairs. With each step, the presence of the entity seemed to magnify. He felt fear, but at the same time an irresistible allure to continue downward. At the bottom of the stairs, he found another door, and knew that this foreign entity must lay behind it. Opening it, he entered into a large circular room all draped in yellow, with an ornate mirror on the adjacent side. He approached the mirror and gazed upon it only to see the face of Lucifer staring back at him. Then he awoke.

"It is an omen," claimed Daimon Fubentronty, "It is a sign that we have lost something, a thing which must be…recovered."

"I must ponder this," said First-Illumined Lucifer, "many questions have arisen for me as a result of this dream. For instance, is there actually some cause behind my own seemingly accidental discovery of the Erbeth? And the synchronicity of us taking up residence in the same neighborhood that Central Authority would eventually decide to establish the human race in? Does this seem a bit **too** coincidental to anyone else, or is it just me?"

All were quiet.

"Fubentronty," Lucifer broke the silence, "You said my dream was a sign of something we have lost…**what** have we lost?

Fubentronty was silent, nervously twisting her tail with clenched fists before finally speaking, "Perhaps it is connected with man and the current state of conflict on Earth? Perhaps we should form a search party, and begin combing the terrestrial regions for clues?"

Another brief silence, then Asmodeus spoke, "Good Prince if I may; As a Man, a Daimon would represent something higher than your self. The dream perhaps indicates that there is a higher aspect to your own existence, something beyond you. However, it must exist within your own realm of possibility, as the force in your dream was still within your own 'house'. The answer lies not outside of you for in your dream, you never had to leave home to seek it. Rather by descending, you discovered unknown aspects of your own foundation. It seems the oracle bids you to seek within and *dig deeply*."

Lucifer pondered these words long and hard. A few days later he would announce his intent to descend into the dark caverns deep below the surface of Mars in order to meditate on the principle of causality. He would also leave explicit instructions that he was to be disturbed only if the firmament of Mars itself were compromised.

The Daimon Belial had also been present for the meeting and like all else was captivated by Lucifer's visions. In the days that followed, he began pondering the question of what it means to 'look within' and how such a thing might be accomplished.

Despite the hazards of wartime, the pull of the mystery eventually compelled him to descend to

Earth to conduct further researches amongst the underground schools and societies there. After a few years of visiting with certain hidden Masters, observing man in his 'natural' conditions, and some occasional bullet dodging, he published his discoveries and conclusions in a book titled "An Anchor for Being". In it he asserted that the practice of spending thirty minutes of every day sitting quietly, relaxing the muscles and sensing ones being, is generally enough to set aright the flow of energies through the body and achieve alignment with both the vertical and horizontal axis' of the cosmic flow of energy. He held this to be true for any being that not already irreparably damaged by a manifestation of the mechanizing systems of Operation Infinite Love. In his concluding chapter, he wrote:

> "This simple practice alone would eventually allow the mind to accurately perceive the universe directly without need for excessive metaphysical assumptions. In fact, in such a state of mind, a decision in favor of life is generally quite easy to identify, appreciate, and carry out. Then, if this same practice is carried out in the company of and in synchronicity with other Beings attuned to a comparable frequency, the transformational effects of the now smoothly flowing Erbeth will be multiplied reciprocally.

> One of the tragedies of the binary manner of thinking instilled in the human thought process, is that the average man's mind will not allow him to believe that liberation is actually so simple a process. His lower emotions and wire-crossed instincts move to unnecessarily complicate the matter, before he is even aware. If he had a wish for higher-being to begin with, he may inadvertently find it has been misdirected into the sea of monotheistic religious fervor, competition over the collection of disposable possessions, or the "March-into-Madness" school of political fervor, idolatry, and war."

His book became a mainstay of theory and practice throughout the fragmenting esoteric schools on Earth, and he attracted his own small group of students. Even after the book was no longer remembered by most, many of his practices and exercises endured with those who continued work in schools.

Belial and his students frequently engaged in what were referred to as "group sittings." Belial and his two greatest pupils would sit with appropriate vertical posture before the class. The class in turn sat facing him with like posture, men on the left side of the room, women on the right. Belial or one of his students would attempt to speak consciously, allowing words of direct experience to well up within and roll of the tongue naturally, in order to effect an atmosphere conducive to maintaining inner attention for all present. This would continue until it was sensed that all were for the most part properly opened and attuned, at which point silent bliss would envelope the room. They would continue to sit in silence, completely motionless, for perhaps two or three hours. Group sittings such as these were carried out no less than twice a week.

One evening, whilst deeply engaged in one of these sessions, Belial encountered something quite unexpected. In the midst of sensing the totality of his being in relation to the vastness of the cosmos, he encountered a blinding flash of energy. As the wave rippled through him, he came to sense he was no longer sitting in the great hall of his school, and opened his eyes.

He found he was standing on the deck of one of the old Angelic Star Cruisers. Next to him was none other than Prince Lucifer.

"Lucifer, my brother! I am so happy to see you again!" Lucifer smiled in return. Belial reached out to embrace him, but found his hand seemed to somehow *move through* Lucifer's body.

"Is this a dream? Have I fallen asleep while sitting?" He queried.

"I don't think so," the Prince responded. "Observe..." he continued as he motioned to the front of the ship. As his eyes followed, he saw to his amazement himself and Lucifer sitting at the control panel. As he shuddered under the queer feeling in the belly that often accompanies the 'out of body' experience, he noted that the Daimons at the control panel resembled the Angelic beings that they once were – prior to the Unknown Celestial Fusion, before they had become themselves Lucifer and Belial.

"No, I don't think this is a dream," Lucifer continued. "I believe rather we are experiencing some sort of displacement phenomenon of space and time. Perhaps a synergetic result of your search for essence, combined with my search for origins. I believe we are witnessing something that happened in the past, before the Fusion; before we were aware of ourselves."

As Belial absorbed these possibilities, the holo-map on the starboard side of the bridge caught his attention. "Look!" he exclaimed, "There's Mars – we're in the Solar System! But where is Earth? And what are we doing here? Had we been to the Solar System prior to the Fusion?"

"I don't know," was the response, "We must have been on some sort of mission for Central Authority. Look – what's that planet between Mars and Jupiter?" As they observed, this foreign body became the focal point on the holo-map, and it became apparent this was their destination. As they settled in to the planet's orbit, they saw a name flash across the map: TIAMAT.

"Alright," the Angelic being that would one day become Lucifer exclaimed from the control panel, "Here we are, the *worst place in the universe*. This is were we dump the garbage." Both began busily manipulating the various knobs and buttons of their control panels.

"Garbage?" exclaimed Belial, "garbage from Sirius? And a planet called Tiamat? I don't understand this at all!"

As they felt the clanging and grinding of the storage bay doors opening from the bottom of the cruiser, they recognized the peculiar scent of ozone.

"The Black Fire!" the Prince of Darkness shuddered. They looked on in silence as the shock and horror realization slowly sank within them. "That's their garbage," mused Lucifer, "Ant it was you and I who brought it to the Sol System." Suddenly the sound of an alarm and red flashing lights broke their reflection.

"Shit!" proclaimed the angelic past-self of Belial, "Something is going wrong...Tiamat...she's breaking up! What do we do?"

"Fuck it!" responded the angelic past-self of Lucifer, "It's not our problem...we did our job...let's get-the-fuck outta here!"

As the cargo bay doors retracted and the ship left orbit, the disembodied Lucifer and Belial looked on in disbelief at the port-side holo-screen. On it they saw the planet called Tiamat breaking up into a thousand pieces. By the time they reached the Solar System's heliosheathe, one of the larger pieces of Tiamat had fallen past Mars and was entering orbit around the Sun in the place where they would one day discover the planet Earth.

And in that moment Belial found himself back in his great hall on Earth, surrounded by his students, all of who were still meditating in peaceful silence. Belial took a deep breath and wiped the sweat from his brow.

In the Martian underworld beneath Saga City Lucifer continued to mediate on his mysterious dream, his encounter with the past, and his question of origins. He was blissfully unaware when some time later the nations of men on Earth finally fired their Solar Cannons, fully destroying three human cities and many hundreds of thousands of Terrestrial Beings. Whether from the sudden death of so many beings, or from an imbalance in the atmosphere caused by the manipulation of Solar waves, this destruction had a secondary effect in that the Earth's second moon - "Amma" – fell out of it's orbit and crashed into the Earth a few days later. Nearly every terrestrial being who hadn't already been destroyed by the Solar Cannon, met their fate here.

While far away Lucifer drifted and swirled amidst the Ancient Dreams, the oceans of Earth swallowed huge masses of land and the dense layer of clouds that had previously protected Earth from extreme heat fluctuations began to vanish.

The Universal Conference of Cosmic Beings

With the opening of the Third Epoch both Angel and Daimon alike were rather distraught by the terrestrial holocaust and lunar catastrophe that had beset the planet Earth. Daimons mourned for the loss of life and their many friends amongst the endearing race of terrestrial hominids. Angels mourned for the sudden loss of an energy source that would now need to be re-cultivated. And so it was decided to call a truce and hold the first Great Universal Conference for all Cosmic Beings, including all Angels, Daimons, Central Authority Agents, Watchers, Emancipators, and everyone else in between who had access to adequate transportation.

First a neutral site had to be decided upon, so a committee formed of Daimonic High Council and Angelic High Council members convened telepathically, first to choose an appropriate site to meet physically, (For it was still a common value among all Cosmic Beings to meet together and exchange directly and in mutual presence whenever possible), and next to appoint a "Peace Keeping Trust" to maintain neutrality on Earth in their respective absences.

The choice for a conference site proved an immense hurdle. They needed a meeting room large enough to accommodate several thousand cosmic beings, plus many insisted on a pleasant climactic location, so that they might be able to entertain themselves between sessions. Further complicating matters, many insisted on reasonable room rates, pleasing amenities, and so forth. In the end, the only place anyone could decide upon was in the Alioth System of the constellation you know as "The Great Bear": Ursa Major.

Next, they set their minds to establishing a peacekeeping force to watch over the precious remaining human lives. This was tricky business, as none of them exactly trusted each other, and it soon became apparent that they might need to retain a neutral party. On the twelfth planet of the Sol System lived a primitive race of bipedal reptiles, called the *Apachana*. The weren't terribly bright, but they were easy to train and competent enough to carry out basic tasks, so long as they were provided with sufficient amounts of a certain ore they found precious – gold. Therefore it was decided to import three tribes of these lizard-folk to Earth in order to a) watch over the humans and ensure no harm come to them, and b) to ensure none of the few remaining Cosmic Beings interfere with human affairs for the duration of the Conference. They were set up with a few small outposts with adequate equipment so that they would be able contact the Conference should any emergencies arise, and watch over the humans at a safe distance.

And so having assured themselves that no aggression would be initiated and no machinations attempted on the small pockets of impoverished humans remaining there, the majority of Cosmic Beings packed their bags, cancelled their newspaper subscriptions, and boarded their star cruisers directly.

Thus it was in a great pentagonal chamber in a popular resort area on Alioth's fifth planet Blohardigan that the conclave of cosmic beings finally took place. Present were the Legion of Angels represented by Ornich, and the Society of Daimons was represented by Asmodeus, and of course no such grand-scaled meeting of the minds could occur without representation for sub-factions, and so for the small Union of Watchers (whom had taken on the unofficial and more mysterious sounding moniker, "The Circle"), was the being called Astaroth, and for the Erbethian Emancipation Movement (or E.E.M.) was Sammael. Even the Angels had created their own singular party – The *World Peace Party* – in the hopes of more bargaining weight.

Introductions took up most of the opening day of the meeting. As nearly the whole conclave was beginning to fidget with yearning, the Arch Angel Michael stood up and called "unfair advantage," pointing out that it was well known that Astaroth and Asmodeus had previously undergone the Sacred Rite of Essential Exchange together, and thus could not be trusted to weigh any of the issues impartially. Asmodeus quickly objected, citing the Daimonic core value of objectivity. Moreover he pointed out that since sexual intercourse was an activity unknown to the Old Race, they had no basis on which to make such a judgment. Soon the entire room was engaged in heated discourse on whether Essential Exchange constitutes 'sex.'

Six weeks later the debate still raged, the 'Human Question' remaining untouched.

Now, any who have ever been made to endure such magisterial cacophony know of the burning desire that may overtake one: to forthwith run with considerable speed away from the fray in search of blessed solitude. It was just this very sensation that consumed and over-powered the Daimon Abrasax, but it was her own subtlety and quiescence that allowed her to slip out of the Great Pentagonal Chamber unnoticed. Intuition guided her down several dimly lit and increasingly uninhabited hallways before a curiously attractive door caught her attention.

"Room 69," she spoke to herself as she read the topaz plaque above the peculiar portal. "Sounds like fun, more fun than a fruitless debate anyhow," she muttered as she opened the door and scanned the room.

While greatly loved by nearly all Daimons, Abrasax had nevertheless acquired a reputation for being a bit of a black sheep within The Society. It was known that she was the daughter of Astaroth and an unknown human, but for most this was the extent of their knowledge, for Astaroth had entered a rather reclusive period during the time of her birth. Always a bit of a rebel, Abrasax had formed herself in a rather androgynous manner, leaving the question of her precise gender a thing of mystery. While some no doubt found this odd, it nevertheless granted her a nonpartisan position within the Society that gave comfort and pleasure to most all who met her.

The adjacent side of her newfound chamber of solitude hosted large French doors to a blacony 6 floors up and overlooking a field of the purple luminescent foliage common to the planet Blohardigan. The doors were standing wide open, and as the glowing vegetable tendrils waved in a rhythmic prehensile motion, their fragrance and light imbued the chamber with a dim electric hue of bluish-violet. Abrasax was drawn to these calming undulations, stepping out onto the balcony to more fully absorb the impressions.

Inhaling deeply, her eyes scanned the serene violet valley. Promptly her peace was broke when she saw on the ground directly below her the figure of an Angel sprawled face-down in the grass. Realizing immediately that the being was in peril and likely injured she hopped off the balcony and glided to his side. He seemed alive, but unconscious, and so hiking him over her shoulder she promptly re-ascended to the balcony.

Laying him carefully on the floor she took a moment to examine the creature, as she'd never before had the opportunity to view one at such a close range -- his smooth and hairless face, his angular features. His glowing white eyes began to open as he regained consciousness.

His first look was of confusion, which turned to interest as his eyes focused on her.

"You're not like the others," he said.

"Are you injured?"

"No, I don't think so," as he began to sit up, "I'm Casmiel," was the sincere and unassuming response, "How are you called?"

"I'm Daimon Abrasax," she said as she rose to face him.

"I thought you might be a Daimon, but there seemed to be something...more. You're...unique."
As he struggled for the words, Abrasax took the opportunity to survey his being. His personality was not defensively armored and constricted in the manner she was accustomed to with Angels, and for perhaps the first time in her awakened life she sensed openness from a member of the Old Race. Her caution turned to curiosity.

"I might say the same of you," was her response, "What were you doing down there in the purple grasses?" At this, Casmiel's demeanor seemed to soften further as he looked down with what seemed like a glimmer of sadness in his eyes, "The din of their voices brought pain to my head. I had to get away from that *fruitless debate*. I was seeking solace when I found this room. I went out on the balcony, and the sound of the purple grasses...so mesmerizing...that's really the last I remember"

Abrasax thought this odd, as she hadn't noticed any sound coming from the grasses. But his sincerity was inspiring, and she vaguely recalled that her people were once like him: asexual and unassuming. "Then I awoke and saw your form...I thought that I had never seen a vision of such beauty. It seemed like somehow, you were a part of it all. You may have saved my life, I am indebted to you."

At this, Abrasax found her forked tongue tied, and could only smile in return. Casmiel seemed to respond with something like a smile, quickly overcome by the sort of expression one makes in encountering a new flavor that is not entirely unpleasant. This resulted in a slight tilting of his head, and for a moment they merely gazed at each other in silence. She began to wonder if anything like this had ever happened before – an Angel submitting to a Daimon. Then she noticed the circular badge on his jacket. "Operation Infinite Love?" she blurted, "are you a propaganda administrator?"

"You might say that."

"I've always wondered," she proceeded realizing she might be at the brink of an amazing opportunity, "How you came up with it? It's so comprehensive, compete and self-sustaining."

"Well, to be honest I was assigned to the project only quite recently. But I do have a clear understanding of the basic principles." Abrasax nodded her head quickly with eagerness. Looking behind her he saw a grease-board on the wall. "It's quite simple really." Moving past her he picked up a marker and began illustrating a pyramidal structure while speaking.

"Once the humans had been tampered with by your kin, we found it was no longer possible to govern them directly. No matter what we tried, they sensed our alien origins, and rejected us as masters. We quickly realized it was necessary to control them indirectly, by means of a system. Thus was created the 'Father Structure.'

"Step One: Establish a family structure centered around the father. Children must be instilled with behavior patterns that are paternally submissive. This is really the hardest part, as it requires that people be indoctrinated into a value systems that encourages abuse and suppression of children, which has the effect of making them obedient in the long-term.

"Of course any father has the option of not raising his children in this manner – he can avoid the cuttings, the punishments, the sexual oppression. But every mother and father wants their children to be socially adept, and that means they have to go to the same schools, cheer for the same teams, and buy their socks at the same stores. His fear...the fear of being ostracized and being rejected, is *so strong*...remember, he *was* a herd beast before you and your crew came along."

"So fear is the main ingredient, and gradual starvation helps too. As humans become increasingly desperate and hungry, they inevitably separate themselves from their emotional centers. Once the ball is rolling, it requires the passage of only five generations before the 'Father Structure' is firmly established and self-perpetuating.

"Step Two: The father structure of the family must be transferred to the social realm. A king of sorts – one of their own kind – must be established to rule over the people. He becomes a father for all the community, and each head of household within that community on this level becomes a child, subservient to the prime father just as his own children are subservient for him. This step can take several hundred years to mature, but does so quite automatically provided no external force disrupts the structure established in Step One. The community of humans will grow, absorbing minor communities and individuals in the immediate vicinity – even those that haven't yet undergone Step One – until such time as it begins to press the boarders of another human community. At this point we consider the community to be matured.

"Step Three: this is the final transition. This same father structure must be transferred to the realm of pure ideas. The *idea* of the father must assume much greater significance than any earthly father, whether a king or head of household. This can be challenging as depending on various regional factors, humans may have some disagreement amongst themselves over what sort of father ideal is believable. Generally the fear of death will bring them together, and this same aspect of the structure – that the father is the true owner of all – prohibits them from creating cosmic bodies on their own. Once multiple kings settle on a common idea, it quickly grows from there by it's own momentum, and there is very little need for us to get directly intervene in the process. It is a self-maintaining system ensuring us with a regular and robust supply of life-force energy for use back in Sirius.

Abrasax was aghast, marveling at so clever and concise a scheme. Then something occurred to her, "Has this same process been applied to your own race? Is your Administrator Prime only an idea? A feature of a system that Central Authority has established for the sake of it's own perpetual maintenance?"

Casmiel opened his mouth as though to respond but then stopped, looking upward and to the left. "You know...I hadn't thought about that before. In fact, now that I think about it, I don't feel so well. Something about those purple grasses."

He began to reel as though he might faint, and quickly the demoness rushed to his side to sturdy him. "Don't worry," she whispered, "whatever it is, we'll figure it out together."

Meanwhile, the conference had made only minute progress. Astaroth had finally consented to removing herself from the Watcher's seat, and the one called Naberius had taken it in her stead. Finally the Human Question was on the table.

All Cosmic Beings seemed to be in agreement that Humans should continue to exist on planet Earth, and this alone marked the limit of their concord. It was the question of Man's function that evoked only controversy. The Legion viewed humankind largely as a commodity – a crop – the Erbethian transformation posing no relevancy whatsoever. The Society generally argued that humanity now served to prove the efficacy of the Erbeth, and that the great experiment could be validated only if humans were allowed the freedom to pursue existence via higher bodies. These words fell as trivialities on Angelic ears. Thus, several more weeks of cacophony emanated from the Great Pentagonal Chamber.

One morning, the first arrivals at session were greeted with a most shocking display: from the high ceiling of the chamber swung a single unhappy Human-Being, suspended from his ankle by a rope, with his hands bound behind his back. Apparently a few mischief-makers had endeavored to demonstrate some point or another, yet none would admit responsibility for the heinous act. This served to agitate the already frustrated conclave, and amidst random calls of "Here is your enlightened being!" and "Who is responsible for this indignation!" the session was soon on the verge of a riot. Conflict was finally averted when out of nowhere the Daimon Beelzebub suddenly burst through the chamber doors, demanding the Conference's attention.

"Who do *you* represent Beelzebub?" Ornich demanded with no small amount of sarcasm, "Emancipator or Watcher?" Emancipationists and Watchers alike looked nervously amongst each other, as no one had actually heard from Beelzebub in quite a while, and didn't really know *what* he'd been up to. Beelzebub's eyes scanned the room in silence for a moment, and then he spoke the words that would become immortalized throughout hundreds of star systems:

"I represent the force of the highest…life."

Even Daimons were indignant at this boast.

"What is this disruption, Beelzebub? Think you we have gathered here for reasons *other* than life?" exclaimed Frimost.

With exacting certitude, he responded, "The question of life has been lost in the Anglo-Daimonic struggle for dominance. Angels, ye act with no knowledge to carry out the sublimation of life in accord with a mandate whose origins even ye have forgotten. And Daimons, ye seek Man's ascendance only to validate your own intersession. What of Man himself? What of life itself? Has it not purpose and function of its own?"

All were silent for a moment, and then at a gesture from the Lord of the Flies, the human was lowered from the ceiling, unbound, and allowed to quickly scurry from the chamber.

The Watcher then gestured toward the door announcing, "Cosmic brethren, I give you the Learned Beings of the Saiph".

In walked four fair-skinned human looking creatures that emanated a dignified purity that was apparent to all. Beelzebub went on to explain that unbeknownst to any but certain Watchers, during the 2nd Epoch, a small quantity of Humans had been transplanted to the Saiph System of Orion in secret. They were provided with all requisite physical and social needs and given sufficient knowledge to begin working with the Erbeth on their own. Over a few short Aeons of peaceful, enlightened, and pleasurable interaction with each other, they remanifested the Erbeth within their themselves to such an extent that they experienced a racial transformation. Their essence-emanations were vibrating at much the same rate as the Daimons and were recognizable as true Cosmic Beings to all present.

Drawing on the example of the Learned Beings of Saiph, Beelzebub proceeded to argue the case that they constituted living proof that the Typhonic Process was a natural life progression possibility, and proof that the Terrestrial Fusion Program was justified. He further argued that since the Human Beings of Saiph were now Cosmic Beings by definition, they were themselves entitled to equal treatment and representation at the Conference.

Many were surprised to see that the Daimon Frimost was the first to voice objection to this. As a conservative of the Watchers Party, he had apparently found resolve in his conservatism that surpassed most of his comrades. "They are the result of Daimonic intervention, therefore upholding Daimonic order should be their lot. They *owe* us." Some Daimons, and Angels, grunted concurrence with this.

Many Emancipationists (who had been at the forefront of the proceedings on behalf of the Socitey) were so taken aback by Frimost's assertion they literally through up their wings in exasperation. Now the question of whether the Learned Beings of Saiph should be allowed representation overtook the sessions, and all were at least vaguely aware that the Conference was very, very, very far away from resolving the 'Human Question.'

After the 23rd week of sessions revolving around the question of what constitutes life and whether humans should be involved in the Human Question, the Conference was interrupted by an urgent hologram from the Terrestrial Peace Keeping Trust. Earth was under attack by savage Extra-Terrestrial creatures and all cosmic beings were asked to return post haste. As all Cosmic Beings of all races and parties scrambled to pack their bags and get their travel papers in order, Abrasax and Casmiel embraced each other desperately once more by the great bay window in room #69

"I cannot bear the thought of returning to Earth without you," she whispered.

"I don't think I could return to my former life, even if I wanted to," he responded, "I am not the same being I was before you taught me the Sacred Rites."

She paused and looked into his eyes, "What are we to do then?"

He looked out the window at the undulating purple grasses. "There is a small moon in a remote sector of Sirius B. It is not of any great consequence to any of my kin, however the soil is much the same as here on Blohardigan. I don't think we would be missed, at least not for a while. As with the Daimonic exodus from Sirius, a few are generally permitted to escape."

And indeed he was right. All that was required was that they sit quietly in room #69 until the Anglo-Daimonic host had vacated. A week later, they were on a small vessel charted for Sirius B with several patches of re-potted purple grasses in the storage hatch. With no apprehension over what the future might bring, they were content merely to be in each other's presence. Happily unaware of the fate of Man on Earth, and happily unaware of their stowaway passenger: a small and unassuming housefly who'd made a home at the base of one of the wavering grass blades.

31 weeks earlier by Objective Time Calculation, or 22,599 years earlier by Terrestrial Time Calculation, the Reptilian Terrestrial Peace Keeping Trust had other things on their minds.

The deluge caused by the cataclysm of Amma had caused the outer layer of clouds surrounding the Earth to dissipate, and men were now able to see the Sun, the Moon, the stars, and were introduced to the pleasant phenomenon of rainbows. Urban civilizations were reforming themselves in the central regions, but the Circle had found greater interest with the remaining humans peppering the rural territories.

One among them, the Watcher called Othil, after paying special attention to key details of the rise and fall of several Terrestrial Civilizations, had come to the conclusion that due to the tendency of humans to store their accumulated information on increasingly disposable mediums (generally for the sake of saving space), and that due to this, every time a comet crashes into the Earth or some army detonates a large-scale explosive device, most of these records are destroyed and the unfortunate survivors are left to interpret what little knowledge remains without a proper context for understanding it.

He further noted that what relevant teachings **did** survive the occasional global destructions more successfully, were teachings that had been passed along via direct contact and the spoken word, and thus they survived with those few individuals who themselves were clever enough or fortunate enough to survive.

Thus, with an eye toward the possibility of Humans having their own self-sustaining system of knowledge, Othil began developing the "Bi'al School", which held that oral tradition is a more durable and accurate means of transmitting knowledge across generations than is any form of recorded matter. The Bi'al School attracted a small group of like-minded Watchers. During their moments of rest from their responsibilities (which were rather menial due to the vast majority of Daimons and Angels having gone to the Alioth System for the Great Conference), they began interacting with Human communities in certain remote or 'rural' areas. In these communities they developed systems whereby man might live in harmony with his natural surroundings and transmit esoteric knowledge orally. The hope was that in so doing not only would knowledge survive occasional mass-destructions more completely, but also that such beings who possessed it would likely be far away from the centers of mass-destruction at the time of their occurrence, as the clouds of devastation tended to gather thickly around the urban centers.

The atmosphere of the Bi'al School promoted much peace and pleasure, and some of the Watchers went so far as taking human wives, husbands, or lovers during this time as well. The fruit of such unions resulted in several new Humanoid species, generally smaller in stature, more reclusive than humans, and physically comprised of finer materials. These were generally called the "Fa'I", and they lived in highly remote areas, enjoying a connection with nature unknown to Humans.

In general the Circle was quite successful in these endeavors. The rural Humans and Fa'I coexisted with each other and their environments with few instances of violence, and a continuous line of knowledge supplied by a rich oral tradition. These streams of spoken knowledge indeed proved to be quite strong, and survived many global catastrophes right up into your own Seventh Epoch. With peaceful and nature loving beings on Earth, and Daimons and Angels light-years away, most of the 3rd Terrestrial Epoch passed in relative quietude. Not as much advancement occurred in the way of science or invention, but the need for such wasn't perceived as necessary to fulfill Being-Duty as had been over the preceding ages.

The First Apocryphal Shock

"Here come one now!" Eridu growled excitedly to his older brother Enki, "Fresh meat fo' tha eatin'!"

Enki's grip tightened on his spear as he glared with intense stillness at the trembling bush in the midst of the apple orchard that he and his partner had been assigned to watch over. Presently a small group of nude anthropomorphic figures emerged from the bushes and began quietly picking apples from the trees.

"GRRRH, is not food, is more hairless human-things!" growled Enki, as he loosened up and sat back down on the large rock which the two Reptilians had made a favorite observation point. From this rock they could see most activities occurring in the valley, and smell even more. Though the humans had been of primary concern in their assignment of maintaining order in the valley, Enki couldn't help but feel a tinge of disappointment every time one of them appeared – they were frail, timid and generally uninteresting. And to top it all off, no only were they forbidden to be used for sport or food, but protecting them from harm was a prime directive. One of this planet's many fur-bearing creatures at least would have promised the opportunity of a good chase, if not a tasty meal. But for these human-things he could see no use whatsoever, and defending them a task well beneath his stature as a Warrior-Prince of Nibiru. Not to mention that no semblance of a threat had appeared in the 526 terrestrial years they'd been assigned here.

But then, who was he to question direct orders and the nature of things?

Enki's frustration quickly dissipated as the yellow rays of the Terran sun warmed his blood against the smooth hot rock. Without even a grunt to his partner, he set down his spear, lay back, and allowed as much of his scaly hide as possible to meld against the rock in pure reptilian ecstasy. Soon he was dreaming of his distant home planet of Nibiru -- of his golden parlor, and his 20 wives, and his 65 hatchlings that would be nearing adulthood now (had they managed to avoid being consumed by their older siblings). Then he dreamt of the golden Thrown of Nibiru, and his father King Anu "The Merciless" scolding him from it.

But before the dream could go entirely bad he was awakened by the sound of Eridu excitedly grunting, hissing, and pointing frantically back in the direction of the grove. But this time it was warranted. A wild pig had emerged from the bushes and was charging full speed toward the dense forest on the western side of the valley. Instinctually both of the two-legged reptilians knew that cutting the beast off before he could make coverage in the forest would result in immediate gratification, and so with a gleeful hiss Enki grabbed his spear and both were off in the blink of an eye.

As they charged full speed toward the pig, both were at least vaguely aware that leaving their post was forbidden. But unannounced visits from King Anu had become so rare on this lazy little planet they gave little worry to the occasional brief 'recreational' abandonment of their lookout post.

Soon it was apparent the beast would enter the woods before they could intercept it. As Enki exerted, pulling a full 8 tail-lengths ahead of Eridu, he contracted and braced himself just in time to vault over a large rotting log and then immediately duck under a low-hanging branch without loosing a step on the pig's trail. He was nearly a tail-length behind and his powerful right arm held spear aloft and ready to thrust when quite unexpectedly, the reptilian hunter found himself rolling and tumbling in darkness.

He was quite stunned when he finally struck bottom of what must have been a rather long vertical corridor leading to the surface. His hands began searching his scaly hide for wounds, as his keen eyes began adjusting to the darkness. He was about to begin cursing the loss of the pig, when the strange surroundings began coming into focus.

Various machines, button panels, and monitors lined the walls of the small square chamber, devices not unlike those he had seen on his father Anu's ship. But what really caught his eye were the curious designs on the smooth stone floor. In fact he was standing right in the middle of an immense white double circle. Around the rim of the circle were painted various characters, unintelligible to him yet vaguely familiar. Soon it dawned on him that this must be an old base belonging to the Winged Ones, the old race that had employed his people to watch this planet in their absence.

Satisfied that he had solved the mystery, he was ready to find the way out and return to his own base to file a report. Looking around for possible exits, he noticed one final curiosity – behind him, right on the perimeter of the circle had been standing a large trapezoidal box. As he approached to inspect it closer he noticed the tall rod leading upward and the five-pointed star-shape within a circle at the top. It had an inexplicably mesmerizing effect on him, and without thinking he reached out to touch the curious device.

No sooner had his horny finger brushed the circular rod than the device began issuing a low hum. Surprised, he took a quick step back and noticed the circular rod atop was beginning to rotate, and a purplish light gradually illuminating the room. Soon he was far too entranced for apprehension, and his surroundings began to melt away into the enveloping purple haze.

No longer was he aware of the device, or the room. In fact, his very own self was **all** he could reckon, and his consciousness was the only limitation by which he could discern his existence. This was all a very new experience for him, as never before had he really considered himself as an individual. He had merely acted in accord with inclination and nature, without reflection or foresight.

He then found himself floating in the limitless serenity of space with only the stars to give him reference. He saw two of the elder Winged Ones floating some distance beyond him, seemingly unable to see him. One seemed to be nursing the other to health, helping him to drink a cup of glowing purple liquid.

Without warning the vision dissipated and he found himself standing in a grayish white desert before the walls of a great city. The immensely high towers shot up into the sky, and the entirety of the city was constructed of glass. Within, he could see more of the winged beings going about their business as one would expect in any city. Then there was the sound of a great bell tolling and all at once every inch of the city exploded into multifaceted shards.

And again he found himself back on the high rock by his observation post looking out over the valley with his brother Enlil by his side. Only now he was dressed in the golden apparel of a king, and out in the valley there were not a small tribe of human-things, but a thousand of them. They were making themselves busy digging up more gold from the earth and slaughtering pigs, all as tribute for Enki. And as he looked behind him a great golden palace reached up to the sky, and on each of the double-doors was carved the shape of an enormous black serpent. He knew that this was Enki's palace.

Then he awoke. He found himself lying on the floor of the dark chamber in the middle of the circle. For a long time he only stared up at the passageway through which he'd fallen, the faint light of day trickling down. He felt very stiff and incredibly hungry, as though he'd been lying there for days. The machine was no longer moving, and all was quiet. He found his way out when looking up through the shaft and noticing the little hand grooves etched into the sides – salvation.

Emerging from shaft, he collected his spear and noted Eridu was nowhere to be seen. A few moments later he emerged from the forest only to freeze in his tracks as he looked toward his outpost on the southern slope of the valley and beheld the enormous draconian styled airship hovering over it.

"Gorilla shit! Father!" He cursed aloud. Immediately breaking into a brisk walk up the hill, he proceeded with a long and colorful steam of curses to himself. "Sure," he thought, "just when I'm inexplicably absent for an indeterminant amount of time, he decides to drop by for a vist." His frustration turned to fear as he saw the figure of King Anu standing upon the slope, hands on hips and eyes fixed in a stern glare. Fear then turned to anger as the figure of his brother Eridu appeared from behind the King. Eridu was obviously trying to hide a smirk and Enki had no trouble imagining that his brother had taken full advantage of his absence by filling his father's head with venom in regard to his oldest son.

Forcing himself into a sense of reverence, he bowed low before his father with a "Hail, oh great King!" Arising, he could see Anu was unmoved.

"Where you been Enki? I leave you hear with easy job to watch frail hairless ape-creatures and you go off to play in forest for days?"

Thinking fast -- in fact somewhat faster than usual -- he responded, "Father, I was conducting research..." stammering, he recalled his visions in the secret chamber, "...on...on these human creatures. They could be a valuable resource to us, yet pine it away as watchmen for the Winged Ones. Why should we protect and serve when it is we who should rule? We who are strong with skins of armor and hands of claw?"

"Silence!" Anu screeched as he clipped the Prince across his jaw, "Winged Ones are strong…elder race…powerful ally to Reptilians! You bad son…don't obey…"

He went on, but Enki could no longer hear him as the powerful visions from the secret chamber replayed in his mind. He began to feel like an outside observer as he noticed his muscles clenching and his spear beginning to rise. He felt no emotion whatsoever in fact, as he watched the tip of his spear plunge succinctly into his father's abdomen, and could only faintly here the startled yelp and subsequent gurgling as blue-black blood streamed forth from his father's lips and trickled down onto his scaly hands, which were still clenched tightly on the shaft of his spear.

No sooner than the body of King Anu had crumpled and fallen to the ground, a mortified Eridu dropped and bowed in acquiescence to his new King. With an aura of pure and prideful majesty, Enki turned to the apple orchard in the valley and saw that a small band of humans had gathered there and had been guardedly watching the proceedings.

"Arise, my brother," spoke Enki at length, "We have great work before us. Be prideful for today we have witnessed the birth of a nation – united in the Age of the Serpent."

"Their society functions under a Monarchical system," explained the Arch Angel Dumaso to his attaché Prumosy, "Their King is a fearsome warrior called Enki. He is the first of seven sons, and it is said that he murdered his own father and consumed his flesh publicly, thus discouraging any sibling rivalry in his ascendance to the throne. For this reason he is revered and feared throughout his kingdom, which he has ruled over now for several millennia."

Prumosy pondered this as their small Sirian landing shuttle passed through the Terrestrial thermosphere and great rolling land-masses came into focus against the contrast of the expansive blue oceans of Earth.

"But why?" he asked, "Why jeopardize our long time partnership for this?"

"As always, they lust for the mineral called 'gold'. They are fascinated by it for some reason. But that doesn't explain what's happening here as there's plenty of gold back on the 12th planet. Enki has cut off communications with home, and they seem mostly glad to be rid of him, so now it's our exclusively our problem. One thing's for certain, the Apachana of Enki's tribe have changed. Their race has always had a penchant for brutishness and selfishness, but they've never before exhibited such ingenuity or imagination as they are now. In a very short time they've managed to develop a relatively advanced system of technology, albeit geared almost exclusively to military and mining interests. They have also developed knowledge of genetics."

"Sounds like another Erbethian intercession. More Daimonic interference?"

"Erbeth possibly, Daimonic interference unlikely according to Arch Director Michael," Dumaso continued, "mainly because of the effect this is having for human life down there…you know how sentimental those bleeding-hearts of the Society can be. Plus they have sworn the Oath of the

Absolute with us to work together at least through the resolution of this crisis. Their engagement of the Reptilian armies to the north may provide us with just the time and distraction we need here, should these negotiations go sour."

"You don't sound terribly confident in diplomacy." His assistant mused.

"Think about it: while we were all busy arguing in the Alioth system, these lizards enslaved what humans they weren't inclined destroy, and set them to work in their gold mines. I should say the *fortunate* humans were put to work in their gold mines; the not so fortunate were eaten or utilized for genetic experimentation. Their main interest in genetics is apparently in creating more efficient and obedient slaves. They've 'inbred' humans over several generations now, which has caused the Sabaoth gene – which I'm sure you recall is the gene that carries the fleshly manifestation of the Erbeth – has vanished from their gene pool. Of course that alone would be a boon for us, and these men indeed have returned to a pre-Ve'p state of beastial intelligence. However they are also losing their ability to procreate, as well as emit an increasingly substandard grade of energy. You know Central can't have that."

"Aggressive lizards, eh?"

"Yes, and with just enough cleverness to make them a threat."

"So…what if the negotiations go sour?"

Dumaso paused for a moment, scanning for the right words. "Michael has said only that the tribute to Enki will be our saving grace. Our mysterious cargo must be left here at all costs. Michael has said that this order comes directly from Central Authority."

"Ah yes, the mystery mineral. What is it anyhow? More gold?"

"No, something else. Something from the Moon."

"But why…"

"He would not say," Dumaso cut him off, "'All will be revealed in time' he said."

An uncomfortable silence weighed on the cabin until finally the great landing-pads of Ur could be seen. "Michael is wise," said Prumosy as he began switching buttons and moving levers for landing procedures, "I'm sure we'll be fine…right?"

"Of course," mumbled Dumaso as the shuttle landed softly on Ziggurat 13, "I have absolute faith in the wisdom of Administrator Prime."

The humans who greeted them were quite docile, if not overly polite. As they walked through the city toward Enki's palace they noticed the city abuzz with humans shuffling through the streets and going about their daily business.

"Where are all the reptiles?" Asked Prumosy.

"They've set up a system where Humans tend their cities, in between mining their gold and serving as cannon fodder for their military exploits. There is a specially bred race of Apachana-Human hybrid – called the Ilu – installed as the middle class to govern the Humans, and the Apachana themselves remain exclusively in their towers. This creates for them even more of a mystic aura in the Human's minds, who fear and obey them diligently."

"Bloody genius," exclaimed the young protégé.

"Indeed, most of these organisms will spend their lives toiling away for masters they will never even see. Observe carefully student of mine, there is much we may learn from these reptiles."

Soon they were at the palace of Enki where they met a number of Ilu statesment and bureaucrats before being ushered into Enki's grand chamber. It was quite a sight, even for two cosmic beings from Sirius. On a great dais sat a reclining couch, and on the couch sat one of the largest anthropomorphic creatures the two had ever seen. He was lying on his belly, whilst two smaller sized Ilu women massaged his back by stepping two and fro. Around him were countless attendants and courtesans, some Ilu and some pure reptile. Food, drink, music, and debauchery filled the grand chamber, and on either side of the chamber were four incredibly large reptilian guardsmen with large spears.

The two angels stood attentively as Enki motioned away his attendants, silenced the court, and rose to a sitting position. "Welcome to Ur, winged ones. What brings you to the palace of Enki!"

"Great Enki," began Dumaso, "We are here on behalf of Central Authority. It has been commanded that you relinquish control of these lands back into the hands of your benefactors," Dumaso noted any semblance of amusement had now completely vanished from Enki's face, and thought he could actually here Prumosy's feathers quivering in fear. Yet mustering his brave face he continued, "We will allow you to remain here and administer, however we must retain full authority, especially wherein it concerns these humans." Enki's face now seemed to exude only anger, and he seemed about ready to pounce. Dumaso continued quickly with the kicker, "As a sign of our good faith and desire to work with you, rather than against you, we bring you these precious stones, mined from our base on the Moon."

Then, two of the attendants that had been following them brought forth the cart filled with shiny silvery ore, wheeled it before Enki, and then quickly scurried off. Enki's demeanor immediately changed to. Slowly he picked up a rock and gave it a slow and careful sniff. Dumaso gave a quick nod of confidence to his protégé before breaking the silence, "It is called Radium, and there are several more tons where this came from. Do we have an agreement?"

With glassy eyes Enki looked at Dumaso and began stroking the sparse hairs on his chin slowly and thoughtfully. "I will tell you a story of my people. Long ago there was a King who loved gold above all things. Once while walking in the forest he came across a rabbit trapped in a bramble thicket. 'Please,' said the rabbit, 'I am really a great djinn, and if you will help me escape I shall grant your wish!' So the King helped the rabbit escape and upon so doing, the creature indeed revealed himself as great and powerful djinn. 'Speak your wish!' he said. 'I wish that everything I should touch would turn into gold.' 'so be it!' said the djinn and disappeared in a puff of smoke. Immediately the King laid his hand on the tree next to him, and sure enough it was immediately transformed into gold.

"The King was full of joy. When he arrived home he began touching everything in his household and turning it to gold. When his wife came in, he was so excited he didn't think twice about touching her before she too was turned into a stature of gold. The same happened when he saw his children. A few days later, all his kingdom and subjects were pure gold. He was truly alone in his golden empire."

Enki paused here thoughtfully. "So...then what happened?" querried Dumaso.

"Why, he lived happily every after," chuckled Enki, as his guards fell upon the two cosmic beings with their spears.

Upon receiving the news, the Universal Conference had immediately turned their attention to resolution of this Earth-crisis. The Conference adjourned, and Angel and Daimon retuned to the Solar System in separate entourages. The Daimons who were now aware of the Fa'I settlements as well the fact that these areas were for the moment untapped by the Apachana, decided it would be wisest to secure these areas first. They did so just as the saurian armies were moving into the extreme northern and southern territories. The Daimons joined forces with the Fa'I lending them their technology to help battle off the advancing Apachana armies.

The Apachana were enamored with the silvery-white metal, admiring it almost as much as gold, and began adorning their inner halls with it. Unknown to them, the radiation emitted from this substance had an even more lethal effect on the sapient reptiles than it did on other forms of terrestrial organisms, and so the Apachana mostly died-off within one terrestrial decade – destroyed by the very object of their obsession. Many of the Human drones and Ilu also suffered ill effects, but managed to survive as groups. After the excessive uranium was removed from the cities and returned to the Moon, the Angels and Daimons conferred again in the city of UR and drafted the Pact of Harmonious Discord. This agreement maintained that Daimons would allow the Angels to continue the cultivation of Humans unimpeded, so long as a precise ration of 23% were allowed to escape and avoid consumption by Central Authority. It was further determined that the Angels would allow for a small symbolic representation of the Society of Daimons within their propaganda, in order to help attract the best candidates for possible escape.

And so Angels maintained authority over the Ilu, who now advanced into positions of state and maintained authority over the Humans. As the Angels began stimulating and micro-managing sexuality and selective breeding in them, Humans indeed began procreating again, and it wasn't long before the energy-economy at Central Authority was back up to speed.

Since this new strain of Humanity -- called "Oscorians" -- had been 'relieved' of the burden of the Sabaoth genes and accentuated self-awareness, the Infinite Love Committee began drafting new protocols for shifting their ideology toward racial hygiene and a strict prohibition of any breeding outside their immediate circles. They had by this time become aware of the gifted Humans remaining in the remote territories, and wanted to keep the Oscorian gene-pool clean and efficient.

And so, Daimon and Angel had actually joined forces to fight the a common enemy. Following the resolution of the crisis, they found a brief coexistence contingent on separatism. A tenuous treaty underscored with awareness that any cooperative effort that had occurred between them would likely be only temporary.

When the hazardous terrestrial conditions produced by the shock of the Fourth Epoch's great crisis finally abated, the love of the various Watchers for their children, the Fa'I, was so strong that nearly all of their races were taken up by the Watchers and transplanted to other systems, the locations of which were kept in strictest confidence by the Circle.

It is worth noting here that many of the Daimons had long admired certain Angelic qualities – their mastery of symmetry, consistency, and regimentation. The Daimons had these same potentials, however the Black Fire had further given them the ability to abstract, self-reflect, and indulge in spontaneity, and so most of their attention leaned toward the artistic, aesthetic, and mysterious. Yet the Great Conference and the Apachana Crisis had the effect of emphasizing some of these commonalities. One result of this was the formation of the School of Symmetry by the Daimon Frimost. Its purpose was to study the Angelic disciplines of mathematics, symmetry, and patterns, in order to enhance the work of the Daimons. After some time, the School of Symmetry concluded that feeling, sensation, and the pursuit of pleasure were all illogical functions, and that the Society of Daimons was being corrupted by entertaining such notions as could not be mathematically accounted for or conceived as absolutes. Frimost attempted pushing certain reforms through the Daimonic High Council, but when these ideas inspired little enthusiasm amongst his peers, he became enraged and resigned from the Society as it is said "in a huff."

The Last Saiphian

When The First Great Universal Conference of Cosmic Beings came to an abrupt and unexpected close, Asmodeus and Astaroth conferred privately, and concluded that for the sake of future cosmic negotiations, they should part company. They decided it would be best for Asmodeus to return to Earth, while Astaroth would return to the Saiph System to dwell amongst the learned beings living there. This teleological suspension of the heart, produced great sadness in both of them, and in a vacant dining area of the conference site they embraced for one last time in the Sacred Rite of Essential Exchange.

And so the Watcher Astaroth left with the Learned Beings from Saiph in order to study their peoples more closely, in hopes of gaining clues as to how Humans might evolve toward their full potential, despite the desperate conditions on Earth.

Due to her sensitivity, compassion, and beauty, it was no great difficulty for Astaroth to integrate into Saiphian culture, and she spent some years there studying and getting to know certain of their accomplished individuals and their circles of family and friends quite well. She learned a great deal regarding the Black Fire and the circumstances under which it may be manifested to its fullest, and this also aroused in her greater empathy for the Human Beings on planet Earth, whom, due to the unhappy conditions there, have many more factors working against the possibility of their mastery of cosmic existence.

But Astaroth was not the only cosmic being whose attention moved to Saiph following the Universal Conference. Certain of the Legion of Angels, who were frustrated by Beelzebub's attempt to bring the Saiphians into the Conference, in league with the Daimon Frimost and some of his students, also began close and careful observations of the beings and culture there, albeit at a safe and undetectable distance.

It was eventually concluded by the Angels of this intelligence-gathering mission that since they had already evolved well beyond the level that their life force energy might be efficiently harvested from them, the Learned Beings of Saiph were expendable as far as Central Authority was concerned. The School of Symmetry further asserted that the Saiphian's existence posed far to many questions regarding the Black Fire. Frimost had invested most of his life in documenting the mathematical properties of the Black Fire, and didn't want to have to rewrite anything.

The Agents communicated these thoughts back to Central Authority, and Central Authority responded efficiently with the redirection of a comet into their planet the impact of which was great enough that their planet began falling into the red Saiphian Sun. Those who were not destroyed by the impact quickly began to suffer from rapid overheating and poisoning of the atmosphere. The clandestine alliance then left the Saiphian system post haste, returning to war ravaged Earth before any there had even noticed their absence.

Astaroth also began making plans to leave. She asked her small circle if any would like to return with her to Earth, where conditions were similar to Saiph, only more socially hazardous. All of them declined. Their manifestation of the Erbeth and consequent mastery of the process of the creation of Higher Bodies left them confident that their individual existences would not be terminated by the destruction of their Planetary Bodies. Only one of the Learned Beings, whose name was Iad, approached Astaroth on this. It should be pointed out here that as their Higher Bodies evolved, the Saiphians had found progressively less cause for procreation, (although no less cause for frequent indulgence in states of ecstasy and euphoria), and so the birth of a child on Saiph was a rare and special event, generally celebrated on a national level. Therefore, it was not terribly extraordinary that there was only one Father with child to respond to Astaroth's offer.

Iad had an only son who was still but an infant, and therefore had not had time or opportunity to create any sort of higher bodies. He thought, if the child were taken to Earth and raised amongst them, he might be better able to deal with the harsh conditions there due to his hereditary Saiphian proclivity for the Black Fire, and as well that in time he might even be able to help some of the unfortunate beings there find higher existence for themselves by virtue of his presence.

Astaroth was happy to oblige, and with the infant named "Iaida" in her arms, she began boarding her ship. With a tear in her eye, she turned to allow him one last look at his biological father. "Cheer up!" said Iad, "It's not the end of the world…just **this** world!" Astaroth answered his words with only a smile before turning to leave. Before she had even returned to the Sol System, Saiph had overheated to the point of breaking-up, and all planetary life there had ceased to exist.

Astaroth arrived back on Earth only a few generations after the Apachana crisis, to find things much changed. Racial mixing had occurred gradually over time between the Fa'I and the Oscorians in the populous areas, resulting in great variation of Sabaoth manifestation in the various peoples of Earth. The pure Fa'I had continued to recede into such small and remote communities that knowledge of their existence in the populous regions became the stuff of myth and legend.

In these same urbanized areas, a new Human empire calling their selves "The Accord" now dominated most of the highly populated terrestrial areas. Their ruling class had descended from the Reptilians, and had mixed blood with the Oscorians to the extent that they were physically almost indistinguishable from humans. With fearful recollection of the Apachana crisis still flowing in the people's blood, they had ironically adopted many of the Apachana customs, and accepted many of their values. Over several generations they had become rather regimented in some of these - for instance the keeping of other humans as slaves, and a ruthless approach to conquering and exploiting territories where other, often peaceful, beings had lived. They also inherited the irrational obsession with possessing the mineral gold, and the practice of eating the flesh of other mammals had become commonplace. Many of the Watchers had expected this, noting the general tendency of primates to imitate their captors.

Astaroth searched among the remote areas till she found an appropriate home for the infant Iaida. Miketh was a Priest of one of the remaining secret Daimonic traditions, and trained in the Bi'al School. He gladly accepted the Daimonic gift of the infant Iaida, and vowed to Astaroth that he would raise the child to the best of his abilities. Astaroth left him with the child, and instructions concerning his origins and the 'special abilities' he might manifest later in his growth, due to the unique circumstances of his birth.

So it was that in the tiny village of Lasham on the eastern periphery of the Accord Empire lived Miketh, his wife Nuah, and their son Iaida. As a teacher of the Bi'al School, Miketh served the function of regional storyteller and healer.

Their son Iaida, had come to them under mysterious circumstances that Miketh was never able to fully describe to his wife or other curious villagers. However since Miketh was wise and kind of heart, and his son was fair and likable, their family situation was never called into question by neighbors. This was perhaps one benefit of living on the periphery of the Empire, as in the more centrally located cities the Accord had strict laws concerning marriage and childbearing. For instance, in the capitol city of Ronuum, it was next to impossible to marry or bear children without first gaining approval and going on file in the state registries. Adoption was practically unheard of outside of the prostitution industry.

Miketh was a kind and loving father to Iaida, and raised him in accordance with what Bi'al teachings had come down to him. Iaida was always encouraged to ask questions, never swaddled as was the custom in the land, and learned how to sit still and maintain good posture at a very early age.

While Iaida was still a boy, Miketh became very ill. When it became clear that he was not to live much longer, he began imparting knowledge to Iadia at an accelerated rate. While he indeed imparted to him much knowledge concerning life and the nature of things, and the significance of Iaida's existence in his own life, he was never able to fully impart the nature of the boy's true origins.

Then, one cold winters day he called him to his bed-side. As his breath was greatly weakened, he beckoned him closer till Iaida's ear was no more than a few inches from is lips. Then he began to speak:

"Though you are my son no doubt, you must know that your blood comes from the worlds beyond. I found you and the way that you came to me is a great mystery. There was a beautiful woman with great wings, long black hair, and golden eyes burning like the sun. She was not from this world. She held out her arms, and I received you."

He paused for a moment as though fully reliving the experience within his being, before continuing, "And even then, fastened around your neck was this sigil."

He opened his hand to reveal a small silver disc, and on it was carved a complex and swirling little design with symbols that Iaida did not recognize, yet felt compelled by.

"Go on, take it. It belongs to you." Said Miketh. Iaida's tiny hand took up the amulet to observe it closer. It was a cold, smooth metallic substance, and the craftsmanship on the carving was more precise than anything he had ever seen before.

"She called herself Astaroth, and that is her sign. With it, you may be able to unlock the mystery of your existence here." He paused then for a moment, and Iaida presently forgot about the amulet as an airy presence began to descend on Miketh. Then ever so softly and gently, he began to sing to the boy.

> *When the question begins to consume you*
> *Like unrelenting flame,*
> *Seek not to relieve yourself*
> *With water or sand,*
> *But allow the mysterious flame to consume you,*
> *For in that burning*
> *You shall for a moment*
> *Come into existence.*
>
> *"I know who I am!"*
> *Cries the liar.*
> *"I know why I'm here!"*
> *Boasts the coward.*
> *"I wish only to be."*
> *Utters the initiate.*
>
> *If you exist*

*The Others may see you.
If you can speak without lying
Then the Others may hear you.
If you can find within yourself a wish
Then the Others may seek you.*

*Stand within the fire,
Stand within the fire.*

As his voice decayed, he had a look in his eye – distant, peaceful, and hopeful. Despite the fact that his mother then quickly ushered they boy out of the room, Iaida was to remember that look many years later, and the words that had preceded it.

Iaida was most sorrowful throughout the years following Miketh's passage, and never felt at peace with it all despite his mother's attempt to integrate him into ordinary society. Unaware of man's possibilities for conscious evolution, death to him seemed only an unjust burden for man.

A few years later, a State-Priest of the Accord came to Lasham to give sermon to the simple villagers there, and thinking this might shake him out if his ennui, Iaida's mother insisted that he attend. The Priest spoke of the immutability of Accord law, and that it could be enforced upon men, even after they had journeyed beyond death. Iaida began thinking that the Priest must therefore be knowledgeable on the subject of life and death. After he finished speaking, there was a silence over the crowd, and then surprise at Iaida's single tiny voice, "why must we die?"

The Priest began to explain how the Emperor of the Accord was only spokesman for the Great Emperor in Heaven, and that the Emperor of Heaven had brought death to man as retribution for his imperfections and his evils. As he chattered on, Iaida became aware that even this apparently learned man did not himself actually know the meaning of life and death, but could only recite such rhetoric and moralities as he had been himself programmed with. Before he had even finished, Iaida had left the crowd to go sit in the hills, and never again did he seek wisdom from the State-Priests who came through the village of Lasham

But even as he became a young man, his questions about the sense and significance of life and death haunted him. Amongst the travelers who journeyed through Lasham he often heard stories of different peoples and different kingdoms to the south, and that there were wise men there, and magicians who trafficked with demons. And so armed only with his walking stick, he left Lasham and his past behind him, to wander the Earth in search of something he could not yet articulate.

After traveling for two days on the great road called Te-Taimo, Iaida met a man who was raving and carrying on as though afflicted with a burning madness.

"I am called Legion...for we are many!" he cried.

"Surely you are ill brother, let me help you." Said Iaida.

"You cannot help me for I am not ill. I'm very learned and have graduated from the great academy in Ur. In fact, I am a wealthy architect!"

But Iaida could see the man wore only a commoner's tunic and was most certainly deluded in his perception of self, and so he approached the man and laid his hands upon him. As he did so he could see into the man, and saw that he was not one person, but actually comprised of many selves. Indeed one of his selves **had** attended school and **was** quite knowledgeable, and yet another was indeed an architect. Another was a loving husband, another a jealous child, another an angry statesmen, and even another that was little more than a drunk and a liar. There seemed to be no end to the personalities vying for control of this man and many of them had quite different and conflicting goals.

Iaida looked beyond them all and found buried beneath, the man's true self – a self that was permanent and connected with his essence. He breathed upon it, and as he did so, all the other personalities contracted and were absorbed by this central 'I'.

He released the man, who inhaled deeply as does an infant when first it emerges from the womb. He looked into Iaida's eyes and said, "I am. Where once I was many, now I am one. I am whole and complete and I can see now that you are indeed a Master. I am called Drakon, and I ask that you take me as your student."

And so Iaida discovered that he had certain abilities not possessed by ordinary men. As Drakon and he continued to travel south on the great road Te-Taimo, they met many other people and soon realized that nearly all of them were afflicted with multiple personalities. Some of them they were able to help, but most were too far afflicted with the madness, and beyond repair. Some of those whom they could help joined them and followed.

The technique for remanifesting a 'permanent I' was something that his students could learn for themselves, and so they could preserve it in themselves and others. Yet none could do it as effectively and effortlessly as could Iaida. His Mastery was unquestioned by all. Thus they began to call him "Idiot," which means: *He who is only his self.*

Iaida cured many people. Many became aware of the disease only after becoming cured, and only then could see how far reaching and devastating it had been to mankind. Some would become convinced that the only reasonable course of action to take was to help rid humanity in general of the affliction, but in all this Iaida found only another question: why? Why was mankind so afflicted, what was the source of the illness, and why did he himself seem somehow immune? Was it connected with his own mysterious origins? His blood from the "worlds beyond" as his father had told him?

It was in pondering these questions that one day he recalled the medallion his father had given him on his deathbed. He began examining it more closely – the queer little lines, half-letters, semi-numbers, dots, dashes and serifs. He began to wonder if in actuality it was some sort of map. After a time, his eyes began to ache with examining the small and intricate lines, and so he decided at once that he must at once produce a larger version of it in order to study it in with greater ease.

The next morning he journeyed alone two leagues into the desert. Finding a smooth wide area nestled amongst the dunes, he drew the sigil in the sand with exacting precision and detail. He then sat down to examine it.

The day passed – then the night, and still he could make no sense of it. In desperation he looked at the medallion once more, and realized he hadn't accounted for the circle of the talisman's edges. With a sudden burst of realization he drew a circle around his map in the sand, and returned to his examination. Eventually night fell again, and he began to nod off.

"Miketh?" He heard a feminine voice. Looking up, he saw a slender female with eyes of gold and hair black as night. He could not be certain that he was not dreaming.

"I am not Miketh," he answered, "I am his son, Iaida. Well...his adopted son anyhow."

She was now looking him over with great interest. "Uncanny," she said, "you resemble him as true flesh and blood. Indeed the heart as great power to mold the flesh."

"To know my father is to know me then. And may I ask who you are?"

"I am the Watcher Astaroth. I am of the Daimonic Race that journeyed to your system from the center of the universe many aeons ago, and it is I who delivered you to this world from your home amongst the Learned Beings of the Saiph System."

"You delivered me from a world of 'learned beings' to a world of sick and deranged lunatics? Might I ask why?"

"Two reasons, my clever god-son: First, because you just might have a chance of making things a *little* bit better down here, at least for a *little* while, for maybe a *few* people. Second, because your world was doomed to die, and the only possibility for saving you was to bring you here."

"Oh...well I guess I should thank you then."

"Yes...I guess you should."

"Ok then...**thanks**."

"No problem." Then there was a slightly uncomfortable silence, which Iaida finally broke.

"Well regarding the first bit, about me being able to make things better down here. I can help people here and there, but the problem is big, really big. How can I change things in a real and permanent way?"

"You must learn to act *passively*", she advised him.

"How is that possible?" he asked, "How can one *actively* change things and remain *passive* at the same time?"

"You must become yourself a passive force, then the right sort of active force – something higher - will act upon **you**. The result will be something higher. Between one and three, there is two. The same principles brought me here to you on this evening."

"Ok," he said cautiously, "but the problem itself, why is it so big? Why is Man – as a race – so incredibly sick?"

Thus the Daimon Astaraoth told the Idiot Iaida the saga of the Cosmic Races, of the discovery of the Erbeth, of the schism amongst the Angels, and of the journey to the Solar System; of the high onyx towers of Mars, and of the wise Prince of Darkness dreamt beneath them. She told him the origins of the Bi'al School and the teachings that had grown from the Black Fire – of the Arachnids who had lamented from it, and the Saurians who had grown power-mad from it. And finally she told him of the days of the Seraphic Wars and of the self-replicating virus of negative emotionality that was born from Operation: Infinite Love.

Iaida had many question for her about himself, the universe, and the nature of man. She answered all of them honestly and to the best of her ability. Finally she said, "And now that you have called me to your world, I am allowed to deliver you. You may return with me now to Mars so that you might see for yourself the black towers of Saga City. You will have full access to our libraries, our elegant halls, and our pleasure domes. The cosmic essence of your adopted father, Miketh, dwells there also."

Iaida thought long and hard on this. At length he spoke, "I cannot leave now. As you said, I may have a chance of making things a little better down here."

"That is fine, I thought you might say that. But be warned, if you should parish before you have completed for yourself the task of creating a cosmic body, your existence will be fully and completely ended as happens with most men. And even if you **do** manage to create a cosmic body for yourself, you may not be able to find your way to Mars or any of our other outposts, and I know that Miketh so longs to see you again."

Several days later Iaida returned from the desert. He informed his fellows that he had learnt the secrets of creating something permanent within man, and that it was time for their work together to progress to the next level – the level beyond human.

They traveled together to the valley called Galveta, and there they established a school. They called it Armoni and there they began work under Iaida's directions -- conducting exercises, studying the human structure, and making wine. They worked without interruption for nearly three years. Then one day, Iaida called his students out to sit with him on a hill-top. In the warm sun of mid-summer, and beneath a clear blue sky he began to speak:

"There are different ways of trying to see the world. Some see it only with their minds, some only with their hearts. This man lives in a world of complexity, another one may live in a world of sorrow. Both live in a creation of their own. If man learns to see with his body, learns to sense and to exist in his body; he will be able to really see into his own heart, and will know that he could wish for nothing higher than to exist and be free. For a moment he will be connected with the highest force in the universe, and he will become himself again.

"But in this same moment, another thing inside of him will appear. A reaction against bliss, a sense that it should not be permitted. It comes not from his true heart, mind, or body. It comes rather from something that has grown, and been cultivated within him. It is called GEDMENTJU and its sign is the Scorpion. Gedmentju has an insatiable appetite and will not stop feeding on your vital energy till you lie rotting in the grave.

"Now, it is possible to deprive this parasitic organ of nourishment; he can be starved out, and will leave you. You ask, but what does Gedmentju want of me? My blood? My flesh? In fact he wants nothing in you that is essential. He feeds rather on bile that is created within you.

"Every man in his life builds around himself a shield. It is called HECATONCHIRUS – the shield of a hundred faces. When he is a baby and he is denied, he builds a little piece of Hecatonchirus. As a child, whenever he is forbidden, beaten or bullied, he makes the shield a little bigger, a little stronger.

When parents become blind with anger, they also help to build the shield. When he is a man, his shield will be very strong, and will reflect many faces. The shield provides many personalities, so that a man can hide from many different enemies. It will keep him safe from others, but it will also hide his true self, even from his own eyes.

"The cosmic fire flows throughout the universe and through man. It contracts and expands with all that it touches. It enters a man when he is still like ice, and then leaves as fire. But Hecatonchirus helps to prevent even the fire from leaving. Some of it remains trapped in the man, and some if it escapes, some even bursting through violently. To direct energy intentionally is nearly impossible with the shield. From this trapped energy the bile begins to form. Gementdju begins to feed.

"So if the shield can be loosened, even fall away all together, cosmic fire will be able to expand, and Gedmentju will leave the body.

"Master?" asked one of his students, "If it is not a naturally occurring organ in the body, then where does Gedmentju come from?"

Iaida stroked his long black moustache in silence for a moment, as if replaying the answer in his head, only trying to determine how best to present it. Then he spoke again.

"It is not a child of this world, rather it is a thing that was brought here by others. You see how man tends his goats? He keeps them within certain boundaries, and then he can subsist off them. It is the same even with bees, or grapes, or grains. You must always remember that every being in the universe feeds off of something, and also exists as food for something else. In the same manner, there were others who wanted to keep man; to subsist off of him. Then Gedmentju was placed there, so that men would not notice what was happening around them, for if they were to realize that they were only food for something else they would likely end their own lives out of despair.

"Things were set up this way a very long time ago. The others are still here, dwelling in the skies, the mountains and cities. Men still feed them with their life-force energy. However, you know that if a goat-herders fence is broken, most of them will not run away anyhow. And even if it is not broken, there is always a chance that a couple may escape anyway. As long as it is only a few, the goat-herders subsistence overall will not be effected. It is the same with man, a few men escape the shield and the others will not notice. But not all men can escape the shield. The others would notice this, and there would be a reaction.

"This is why, my brothers and sisters, when you come to me saying that we must tell the world of this way of freedom, I become grim. There can be no such thing as freedom for everyone, without a price so heavy this planet could not continue to maintain its course. If you remember anything ever that I have said, remember this: only the few may escape."

All were silent for a moment, and then another younger student asked, "Is it then man's true purpose in the universe to serve only as food? If this is our true purpose, then what right have we to escape?"

"You will recall the red cosmic fire which touches all things in the universe and pulsates at a frequency that allows for organic matter to exist;

there is another substance in the universe that is called the black fire. When connecting to an organism that has become properly receptive, it combines with the cosmic fire and allows the organism to be able to perceive and appreciate both red and black fire. Once, a million generations ago, this black fire came to an ancient race. They found that their essential existence could be enhanced, by passing the black fire along to yet another race. They in turn passed it down to another, and so on until the result was you and I, sitting here together on this hill-top."

All were quiet for a moment. Off in the distance was the screech of an owl.

"The cosmic fire moves in a great cycle. A charge moves upwards with creative potential, until it reaches a certain capacity and carries the energy for a while. Then it discharges mechanical potential, which falls back downward where it joins the energy level of the environment. An organism that can perceive the black fire, may also be able to observe this cycle, and even make certain adjustments to it. This makes men and women like us one of the most powerful organic beings in the universe.

"The others, who came from the moon, were hungry and wanted to feed from this energy. They released the parasitic organ to man, which makes it very hard for man to be able to see the black fire. But man does have the right to be able to see this, for the black fire hath given it purpose. The black fire is in itself, purpose."

In the months that followed, many students thought long and hard on these words. They came to work in increasing silence, and found they could understand each other much more clearly. They worried less about the state of mankind, and found more time for creative work. Occasionally a traveler would stop by and they would offer him bread and wine. Some were curious about what they saw or heard amongst the group, and some of these would even ask to stay and work. Once even a group of Accord Soldiers stopped by on a mission, and even these were offered wine and bread, leaving in much good spirit.

One day a young man called Stopheles came to the Armoni compound. Dressed all in black and red, he bore the distinctive aura of a Magician, and carried a walking stick with a bronze serpent's head atop it. He said that he had heard there was a great teacher here, and he wished to meet him. Iaida welcomed him in for dinner, which the household was busy preparing.

As Stopheles sat alone in the parlor, he could hear the sounds of dinner preparation – the clinking of dishes, the shuffling of feet, and the pouring of water. All quite normal, but something about it struck him as odd. At length he realized what it was – the distinctive absence of speech. The students were orderly moving about in complete silence preparing the evening meal. "How odd," he thought to himself. He began to wonder if these students took a vow of silence, but this theory was promptly rejected when an older female student appeared in the parlor stating, "Dinner is served, Mr. Stopheles."

They all sat down a long table in a humble dining room, Iaida at the head of the table. The table had been set with great care and precision, and the variety of meat and vegetable dishes was a delight to the senses. There was a momentary silence, and Stopheles began to grow slightly uncomfortable with anticipation. Most of the students were looking down, some even had their eyes closed, but Iaida was looking around at everybody with his piercing dark eyes. His eyes fixed on Stopheles, who returned his gaze with a perfunctory nod of acknowledgement. Iaida did not respond to this, only kept his gaze fixed. Subordinately, Stopheles turned his attention back to the table arrangement.

At length Iaida returned his attention to the table and began to speak.

"All seekers of truth must remember that you are what you eat, and there are many different kinds of food. There is meat, bread, and wine to feed the body, and there is breath to feed the heart. What few realize though is that ideas are also a kind of food. Not only the ideas themselves, but also the way in which they are received, go into making you what you are. Therefore, it behooves every man to be conscious and mindful of the ideas and images they receive. A thing cannot be born from no-thing, but only as a result of transformation of raw materials. There is in fact no such thing as nothing. All is present. Now let us enjoy this meal".

At this the students began passing around dishes and eating with great zest. But still none spoke, focused only on the task at hand. For some reason Stopheles found his self increasingly agitated by the silence, and unable to eat he began speaking.

"I have come from the City of Ronoomb where I was initiated into the mysteries of the Temple of Dalete. There I learned the secrets of the Black Flame and advanced to the degree of Master. Then I found there were none who could teach me any further, and so I set out to seek Dalete himself, the Father of Darkness, he who granted us the Black

Fire. Many travelers I met along the way, and many spoke of Iaida of Armoni Valley and his remarkable teachings. I found my way here, to ask that I might join your school. There is surely much I can teach you in turn that I have learned from the city temple."

A brief clank of dishes and then a blanket of silence as all at the table froze looking downward. All except Iaida, who continued to eat for a moment, and then stopped and said, "You seek outside of yourself, when you should seek within. But perhaps there is yet hope for you," he said stroking his moustache and looking thoughtfully at the urban black magician, "We have an irrigation ditch on the western hill that is only half completed. Finish the ditch, and you will be accepted into Aromoni."

The next morning, Stopheles went out to view the task. As he surveyed the land, he was quickly aware that it would take at least a month of work for one man to complete the canal. "This can't be right," he said to Iaida, "I offer you knowledge, and you demand a peasant's toil from me?"

"Work qualifies existence," said Iaida, as he tossed him a shovel, "When you are able to qualify your existence by your effort – rather than by your words – then you will be prepared to meet your 'Father."

Indignantly, Stopheles began digging. At the end of the day he was given a humble meal of bread, lentils, and wine; and then shown to his quarters: a 10' by 10' room with only a straw mat on the floor and a small table with a candle. As he laid there in the dark noticing every sore muscle and nerve in his body, he felt as though his existence were little more than a large, clenched monkey's fist. Yet he vowed to himself that he would accomplish whatever task was demanded of him in order to obtain the initiatory secrets of Armoni.

The next day all the students of Armoni rose at sunrise and busied themselves with the days work. Minding the vineyards, tending the small collection of livestock, cleaning the house and so forth. Iaida the Idiot was nowhere to be seen. Without even attempting to speak to anyone, Stopheles returned to his ditch and resumed digging.

Occasionally, at unpredictable intervals, a student would emerge from the house and ring the bell that hung from a post in the front yard. Whenever this occurred, all of the students – no matter what sort of activity they were engaged in – would literally freeze their movement. Even those whose bodies may have been in a particularly uncomfortable position would conform to this rigid stoppage of movement. After a few seconds, the bell would ring again, and they would continue their activities as though nothing had happened. Stopheles could make no sense at all of this bizarre ritual, but by the third ring he began 'stopping' along with them.

At noon there was a final bell and they all immediately dropped whatever they were doing and gathered in the main house, which subsequently emitted the quiet clanking of dishes and delightfully appetizing fragrances. One of the students brought Stopheles some bread and grapes, and a bowl of water. Without a word she then joined the others. Stifling a small 'hrumpf,' he sat down and began gnawing on the crust of bread.

As he returned to his task, he noticed the students leaving the main hall, and entering the slightly larger facility next to it. For about an hour there were no further signs of activity, and he began wondering what they might be doing. As he continued digging, he presently heard the sound of music emanating from the structure, of curious stringed instruments. Softly, the sound of their voices began to rise, and he strained to hear what they were saying. They seemed to be counting in rhythm to the music, but in some sort of queer sequence making no apparent sense. This continued for roughly another hour before ceasing. Then the music stopped and all seemed quiet except for an occasional lone speaker's voice, but it was far too faint to be audible.

A couple of hours later the students all emerged, running about putting finishing touches on the days work – much of which had been dropped in a state of partial-completion at lunch. Then they all gathered in a group and Iaida leading the way, marched off toward the hills to the east. Stopheles continued digging, despite the inner struggle that was arising in him. Several times he thought earnestly of dropping the shovel right there and returning to Ronoomb, but some wish to know the meaning behind these curious routines kept him there.

As dusk began to fall, the group returned. The women went into the house where they were apparently preparing the evening meal. A group of men congregated on the porch where they appeared to be unwinding, smoking pipes and speaking softly. With light fading, Stopheles presumed he couldn't be expected to continue digging, so he laid down his shovel and approached the men.

They saw him approaching but made no gestures of acknowledgement nor spoke any words.

He sat down on the step a few feet away. The men continued smoking in silence. Presently, one offered him a pipe, and he accepted. As he inhaled deeply a sense of having accomplished something other than ditch digging seemed to pervade his aching body, and for a moment he almost felt as if he belonged there. But then a female voice from inside informed them that they were ready, and the men all got up at once and entered the house. Stopheles decided to follow.

The scene in the dining room was much as it had been the night before, the students all sitting quietly, Iaida at the head of the table. Presently, Iaida began to speak:

"Every organism in the universe must eat something, and every organism in the universe must also serve as food for something else. Everything thing you take into your self – food, water, air, energies, even ideas and images – all go into building what you are. This in turn determines what sort of food you will be for others. So you see you do have some choice in the matter – you could produce grape juice, but why do this when you *could* produce wine?

"It is very important then, in the work of unifying the self, that you become mindful of what you eat, especially in regards to the impressions that you consume. There is a great division within man – all of you have perceived this within yourselves, or else you never would have come here.

"Nearly all esoteric systems that exist have grown out of this essential apprehension of an internal schism within the self. The random shocks that life provides us will cause even the most dense of humans to awaken for a moment and sense this inner struggle. It may be interpreted as a duality of the body and the mind, or perhaps they will see that the self is really a multiplicity of personalities. And so it is inevitable that some men will begin to wish for some sort of inner unification.

"And so the next step is that a model for inner unification is developed. For instance, the Emperor of the Heavens is one such model. He is said to be the creator of all things and the maker of all laws. He is always right in all his thoughts and deeds, and never experiences doubt or regret. All men wish somewhere deep inside them that they could be like this.

"The next step is that a *system* develops around this. The various stories and rituals surrounding the Emperor of the Heavens may have once been such a system. In order to work toward unity man needs things to do, for his interactions in the outer world will give him clues to understanding his inner world.

"This is where things start to go horribly wrong with most systems. As men begin working with the myths and rituals, they begin to look increasingly outside of themselves for answers. This is especially true if there are greedy or unscrupulous people leading them. In looking outside of themselves for truth, they only reinforce the internal schism, and forget that truth is really inside.

"But still they will long for unity, and in an effort to replicate that sense they will begin trying to create it in the outer world. To do this it is of course necessary to get everyone in your family, your town, or your country to be in agreement on the same model. In these parts, again it is the myth of the Emperor of the Heavens that has prevailed as the state religion. But again, as men are obligated to look outside themselves for truth their inner schism will only be reinforced, not only for themselves but for all their posterity as well.

"Therefore, in order to really make any sort of progress toward healing you inner schism, and begin taking an active role in controlling what sort of food and impressions you consume, it is necessary to break away from the mainstream. You may even have to allow strife in your family, which will want you to reinforce the dominant mythology of external unity."

Here there was a long pause as Iaida looked around the table at everyone. All kept their gazes down, pondering deeply on the words until finally the Idiot spoke again:

"Enjoy your food."

And so things continued in much the same manner each day that followed. After two weeks, Stopheles completed his ditch, and joined the other students' routines – keeping up the grounds, preparing meals, learning the sacred dances of the Bi'al, practicing exercises geared toward the development of self-consciousness, and listening to Iaida's talks. The weeks became years, and in time he grew to be one of the Great Idiot's favorites.

But while Iaida continued experiencing moments of satisfaction that he was helping mankind, he could not ignore a growing pang of frustration. For though it seemed on the surface that his small group of seekers were actually developing something real and permanent inside of themselves, if one looked a little deeper it was difficult to say whether they had only developed the ability to mimic *the appearance* of one who has something real and permanent in themselves.

This was a most disturbing notion for the Idiot. He had always expected that once someone had developed a unified self, a school such as this would no longer be necessary. After all, once one is cured of typhoid or consumption, one spends no excessive time hanging around the infirmary. He began to wonder if perhaps some of his advanced students needed only a little push, much as a fledgling sparrow needs only a little push from it's father to leave the nest and begin flying.

So over the next few weeks he began changing the angle of his talks. Rather than emphasize introspection and practical work, he emphasized the need for autonomy, courage, and sovereignty. He drew upon the archetype of the great warrior, extolling the virtues of pure independence and warning that a man is not a *real* man unless he has delivered himself in the end by his own efforts and will.

While this seemed to get the students somewhat excited, several months later he founded himself yet surrounded by his flock. So he decided to take it up a notch, and started explaining that eventually leaving the group could in fact be part of the "destiny of true will" that might be unlocked through initiatory work.

The curious result of this was that some of the students began stating that they had discovered their true will was to stay in the school, so that they might help others. Before long all the students were reflecting this same sentiment.

In increasing frustration, Iaida came to the unavoidable conclusion that something was going quite wrong with his work, and that a radical solution was immediately required. Therefore one morning he called all his students to meet him out on the porch.

"For most of you, your presence here at Armoni has become entirely futile! I cannot work with any of you any longer and you must all vacate immediately!"

They all sat in silence. "You think I'm joking?" He continued to rant, "You think this is some kind of test? You'd be wrong. I'm dead serious! Each and everyone one of you, get your stuff and get the Hell out of here...NOW!!!"

Still he received only silence and puzzled looks in return. He noticed that some seemed to be looking toward Stopheles, as if waiting to see his response. Then Stopheles began to speak in a calm voice, "Great Idiot, *you* have taught us the inestimable freedom that comes from pure dedication to the work. Never again could we walk the paths of the profane."

Iaida's face was starting to get red. In a flash he realized that the only way to help them get past the final barrier to true freedom was to remove himself from the situation by his own hand. "Well to Hell with all of you then." He said before storming off into the woods.

Through the hills to the east he wondered until he came to the great mountain called Threshold. He climbed to the top where he found a cave, and this he made his new home. For several years he dwelt there in solitude. As time went on, he reflected. The essence of the mountain – with it's solidity, elevation, and continuity – somehow became a new teacher to him. The question of man's mass psychosis and possible evolution paled in the background of the subtle teachings of Threshold.

Eventually he began talking to the mountain, and it – in some ineffable manner – began talking back.

As his mind discovered further freedom from the confines of time and space his perceptivity grew in like, and from time to time he would look in on the events in the surrounding lands without ever physically leaving the sanctuary of Threshold. And of course he couldn't resist looking in on Armoni from time to time.

He was not surprised when he saw that Stopheles quickly emerged as the new leader of the school. He was not surprised because for the most part he no longer particularly cared, and given the man's background in urban religious movements he had always considered that some degree of power-lust was to be expected.

Five years passed before he thought to look in on his old school once more. He noted more changes: the students had all adorned matching tunics of blue. They practiced curious variations on their old exercises and sacred dances, which now seemed rather regimented and focused almost exclusively on emotional work. Well, it was not so much like work he figured, but more like group catharsis. In addition to their wine production they now also had set up production of books, presumably regarding the teaching, and selling these as well. Even wagons full of books would leave Armoni with Accord sources, and so Iaida speculated that the teaching must have become horribly perverted if it were now accepted by the state.

Yet still he was not perturbed. He wondered in fact if this was not the ultimate result of attempting to give men possibilities for conscious evolution –

that in the end even the most enlightened teachings are doomed to perversion at the hands of the greedy and at the expense of the meek.

Three more years passed sleepily on Mt. Threshold and Iaida had all but forgotten his previous life as a prophet. He may have dwelt there in harmony to the end of his days but for an unexpected intrusion upon his bliss.

And indeed this time he was surprised to see Ennos, Cryptonimus and Lucien – three of his prized students from the old days – appear beaten and frazzled on his high plateau.

"My dear children, what brings you to this lonely place?"

"Master," responded Ennos, as the three all bowed in synchronicity, "we have come to entreat upon you to return to Armoni for the situation there has grown most dire."

Iaida recalled for a moment that in the old days, he would have first insisted they drink tea with him or engage in some other such mundane activity before allowing them to speak so that they might collect themselves carefully prior to revealing. But their sense of urgency seemed so great he only nodded for them to continue.

They explained to him how in his absence, Stopheles had gained control of the school and perverted Iaida's teachings into a monotheistic myth system that shackles the emotions and makes men easy to control. He had inserted into the system, his old Temple of Dalete model of a non-material 'father of the flame,' as well as most of the customs of Accord state religion. This had brought them financial support from the government, and coffers of Armoni had swelled to Stopheles' benefit.

At none of this was Iaida surprised. He said, "My children, all these things I have seen from my sanctuary here. While it may sadden my heart, I tell you now there is not a thing in the universe that you, I or anyone else can do to help someone who does not wish for it. A man may help only himself, as you three have done in coming here. If you wish to continue the great work here with me you are welcome, and I shall show you all the great secrets that this mountain has taught me. But you must forget about the others. For them there is no hope."

They were silent here for a moment, and glanced at each other as though to say they wished that it were only that simple.

"Master," continued Ennos, "State support brought with it a price that is grave. With his knowledge of the archane, Stopheles has constructed a weapon. A weapon that uses the Erbeth to manipulate the environment, accumulate and direct energy from the atmosphere, and wreak terrible damage upon the enemies of Accord. Even now he prepares to use it on the hordes of Serpent-Men who emerged on the Southern shores 3 days ago."

The Great Idiot's eyes grew wide and his skin paled as the idea of the Erbeth harnessed for the purposed of mutually reciprocal destruction for personal profit sank within him. At the same time anger and regret welled up within him, for having ever allowed Stopheles into his school.

"Well then," he spoke at length, "we must end this. The only chance of avoiding disaster lies in destroying Stopheles. I must encounter him alone, it would be dangerous for the three of you to be there – his influence is still buried within you, and he may turn you against your will. You should remain here.

Even if I do not return from this confrontation you should remain here, for it is a sacred place, and in my cave you will find instructions for how you might remanifest our work."

"But Master," said Ennos, "you speak as though you may not return?"

"Do not be afraid," said the great Idiot, who now seemed to radiate an inner light of strength and comfort, "Everything returns."

"My children, the hour of reckoning is here!" Stopheles shouted to the grand assembly of students, priests, Accord guards, and state officials. The air was immediately filled with the roar of cheers and shouts and salutes as the assembly looked on with awe at the great structure behind the demagogue.

An elongated trapezoidal structure, easily a 100 meters tall, shot up into the sky. Its shiny black surface reflected the skies above, and from its top shot forth silvery twin antennae, reaching forth another 12 yards.

"By the grace of the Unseen Father, we have received this: **The Holy Tower of Regret!**" Another wave of cheers and applause rolled over the assembly.

"Our ancestral enemies, the Children of the Serpent have arisen from the depths to march upon us and reclaim this land for themselves. Is it any wonder that the Father has sent us this Holy Tower now, in our greatest hour of need? No I say, it is only by the Father's infinite love for his children that we are to be delivered. By the Tower of Regret we shall call down all of our Father's wrath, and strike down our enemies and all who would stand against our noble race!

The next wave of raucousness was interrupted by the sudden appearance of another figure on the podium. "Hello my old student," Iaida addressed the demagogue, "So this is your greatest achievement, a weapon of mass destruction? What happened to that grail of truth you once sought?"

Stopheles overcame his surprise quickly, "Why Iaida, what would you have me do? After all it was you who abandoned your flock, and all I have done is taken responsibility for their protection. That you lacked the courage to utilize the Erbeth to its full potential is no one's fault but your own."

"Full potential?" said Iaida, "is that what you call this machine? Did I not teach you that the greatest potential lies within, not without? You have no idea what sort of force your dealing with, and once unleashed you'll be unable to restrain it!"

Stopheles was silent for a moment, and it almost seemed as though he were remembering some long-forgotten sensation. Then the look of exaggerated confidence returned, and he shouted, "Enough! I grow weary of your condescension!" And in a flash he transformed himself into a Blue Jay and flew up toward the top of the tower. Seconds later the cloud witnessed a second flash, and where Iaida had stood a small red Cardinal flew up after the Blue Jay.

"It's too late, Iaida!" the Blue Jay whistled, "Even if you could overpower me, you cannot stop the great unleashing that is doomed to occur. Another would take my place, then another, and then another. You would have to yourself become a perpetual Minister of Death in order to prevent this!"

Iaida tried to disregard these words although something in his heart recognized the glimmer of an unhappy truth.

Arriving at the top he resumed his human form to face the rogue student, his gray robes billowing in the wind in rhythm with Stopheles' black and red tunic. "And would you like to know why, old master?" he continued pejoratively, "Because that in the end is what people want – to be told what to do. They don't want to learn what's right for themselves, the path to self-unification, or how to live forever. No, their collective will is far more modest than you probably ever imagined. All these people really want is to be told what's right and know the clear path to obedience."

"Foolish boy!" retorted the Iaida, "Therein lies the key of your own downfall, that you toil over what 'the people' want, looking always outside of yourself whether it be for power or for approval. All that has grown within you is your lust for result! I now am thankful that never was revealed to you the full extent of my knowledge! Now you shall receive your final lesson in the Erbethian process!"

Stopheles became aware that the skies had darkened with clouds, and that a swirling blue-grey mist was accumulating on the tower and rolling off over the sides, and for the first time in many years he began to feel unsure of himself. He looked again at Iaida who now seemed to be hovering just above the layer of mist. His face was changing, or rather something 'behind' his face was emerging. It was a face not of this Earth, an eldritch being who's eyes shown with an awareness that could originate only from beyond the stars. Without thinking, Stopheles cried out in terror.

And once again, Iaida felt his heart pierced. Not by thought or deed this time, but by the cold steel tip of a Accord arrow. Both magicians stood locked in each others gaze for a moment suspended in time. "Observe well little brother," the Prophet spoke softly, "for this is my last lesson for the people of Earth." And then the Master Idiot's body fell slowly backwards from the Tower and plummeted into the madding crowd below.

Atop mount Threshold, Ennos, Cryptonimus and Lucien had maintained vigil. As time passed, the skies to the west had become increasingly dark and turbulent, and still Iaida had not returned. Thus were they becoming increasingly nervous about the situation at Armoni.

"He's in trouble, I can feel it," said Ennos, "we should go back and help."

"No!" refuted Lucien, "he charged us to remain here, and remain here we must. Should he not return we must continue the work here."

"But what if he has met ill fate?" Interjected Cryptonimus, "how can we continue the work with out a Master's guidance?"

"*I have returned*," a new yet familiar voice surprised them from behind. They all swung round to see hovering by the mouth of the cave, a luminous being that shown of brilliant golden light that was a strain to look upon. Though not bearing any of the particular lines and features of the being they had known was Iaida, they nonetheless could recognize the essence of the Great Idiot.

"My work here is done my friends. Though not myself of this world, I have watched your race for many years, and know that the pain and suffering and contradictions of your existence are not entirely your own fault. But I have returned to remind you that the way to overcoming them is a burden for your own shoulders.

"At certain moments, the universe opens up certain windows and doorways, and if you are prepared you may be able to see through, or even move through them. Remain vigilant in your search, and you will find the source."

And then a great disc of fire descended slowly from the sky. It made a sound like the baying of a thousand jackals, and the three initiates were terrified to look upon it. But in that moment each of them knew the truth of his words, that his origins were not of this world, and that there was a possibility for existence beyond this world.

The fiery red disc took Iaida up into it, and disappeared into the heavens. Soon all they could hear was the sound of thunder to the west, and felt the violent winds of a storm approaching. Quickly they ran to the cave to take shelter.

High above in Astaroth's space ship Iaida looked down upon the shiny blue plant. He saw the Tower of Regret pulling the cosmic Erbeth from the atmosphere and generating violent wind and rains. Then 2 great bolts of blue lightning shot forth from Regret's dual antennae, streaking over the lands and impacting the coastline. Within a few moments the entirety of the Serpent-Man horde was decimated.

Yet the winds continued to blow harder, and the blue lightning continued flickering around the lands. Soon another bolt shot forth in what appeared to be a random direction, then another, and Iaida was not the only one who could perceive that something had gone terribly wrong with the master-weapon called Regret.

A few moments later and the land as far as the eye could see was bathed in dancing blue voltage, scorching the earth and all it's inhabitants without mercy or discrimination.

Silently, Iaida switched off the view-screen and spoke, "Mother...I've failed."

The Trans-Dimensional Pipeline

As the Fifth Epoch ended in a merciless storm of electricity, wind and flame, the three beneficiaries of Iaida's teachings found themselves in the unprecedented position of having to decide how best to reconstruct the teaching to the culled populous of a desiccated land. Iaida's last lesson was not wasted on them, and they began collecting survivors.

Eventually they split into three groups – the first led by Lucien set sail to the West, across the waters until they found a large island in the middle of a vast ocean that was unknown to any of the "civilized" world. They called it "Atapa," and they became known as the **School of Movement**; seeking to approach the Erbeth by means of ceremony, sacred dances, and work with vibrations and geometry.

After several generations, some of them began to experience changes in their genetic structures, such as their hip-bones eventually rotated 180 degrees, which made it much easier for them to exist in water. Eventually, they split into two races, and the "Dapi" – who eventually had lost all their hair and developed fins, left land altogether to live in the seas. The remaining continued their work as land-dwellers, but occasionally they would meet up in boats with the Dapi to exchange ideas and experiences. In this manner, they gained a significant amount of knowledge regarding the world beneath the waters.

The second led by Ennos also set sail but to the South where they found an island at the polar cap, which in the Fifth Epoch was not yet iced over, and still quite habitable. They became the **School of Vision**, and their methodology involved training the mind to be able to see reality accurately, so that the Erbeth might be approached directly. Recording experiences via various mediums and knowledge of Terrestrial as well as Cosmic events and beings constituted a large amount of their work. Their symbol was a triangle.

After several generations, their genetic composition also underwent a series of mutations, until a third eye appeared on their foreheads. This allowed them to perceive four-dimensional space, and so their ability to remember the future was greatly enhanced – an uncommon ability, even among Cosmic Beings. Their peoples came to be called the "Ooaona."

The third group with Cryptonimus remained stationed on Mt. Threshold, and came to inhabit the various caves in the surrounding mountainous regions. They intentionally avoided taking a name or symbol, but the Daimons took to calling them the **School of Aletheia**. They attempted to approach the Erbeth by 'feeling' it – within as well as beyond themselves. They also worked heavily with essential exchange between initiates, and discovered the immense benefits that might be derived from this. They also studied the principles of music very intensively and recorded whole histories and initiatory manuals in the form of song.

After several generations, these beings also underwent a genetic mutation, resulting in individuals possessing four, six, or sometimes even eight arms. They also developed the ability to communicate entirely by feeling, empathy, and music so that eventually ordinary speech was no longer utilized. Many of their generations enjoyed euphoria and solitude in their mountain paradise.

The few other men who had survived the devastation knew nothing of euphoria or solitude. There was much disease and strange new beasts appeared on the Earth. Those few remaining men lived mostly as brutal savages. Most areas of the Earth experienced extreme desiccation, and due to the extreme lack of vegetation men became mostly carnivorous. As their numbers gradually increased over generations they again took up the practices of war, exploitation, and in some areas cannibalism. Throughout the entire Sixth Epoch these profane men never evolved far beyond stone-age technology. They never ventured across the seas either, nor into the mountains, and this allowed the Iaidic Schools not only to remain intact, but also to progress to the genetically transformational levels mentioned.

Up high in the onyx towers of Mars, the Daimons watched these terrestrial events with great interest. They noted that the Angelic race's attention had become exclusively focused on the masses of barbaric men, and they seemed either unaware of or indifferent to the remote Esoteric Schools. Many of the Daimons again took up traffic with these schools, and found an exchange of great benefit to both Cosmic as well as Planetary Being. Many of the Daimons also again turned to their own studies and projects, many of which had been left in a state of incompletion since the close of the First Epoch.

For Iaida, life on Mars afforded him entirely new perspectives on the problems conscious evolution on Earth. He wrote on these extensively in his book *Socio-Political Equilibrium on the Planet Earth.* His central theme was that esoteric knowledge may exist only in small quantities in order to remain potent. This was called the Law of Qualitative Inversion, holding that if esoteric knowledge is spread too widely it becomes diluted and ineffectual. In short, quantity is increased only at the expense of quality. He further noted the historical trend that if esoteric schools themselves become too large, it tends to provoke a hostile reaction from mechanical forces, and thus all genuine esoteric schools must consign themselves to existing as a small and hidden minority. His book was widely read by initiates on Mars as well as Earth, and considered by many to be the most significant book to be published since Belial's *An Anchor for Being.* To be sure, his Law of Qualitative Inversion became a standard of Daimonic foreign policy.

At one point in this period during a Daimonic envoy's visit to the School of the Aletheia, the Daimon Asmodeus became so entranced by the melodies and rhythms of the school that he decided to remain on Earth and continue studies with them. After much work and research, and in collaboration with initiates of the school, he invented a revolutionary new musical instrument called the Xenotron. Supported by central beam extending to waist-high, the device sported nine metal rods, attuned to the seven notes of the musical scale and the two shocks necessary to complete an octave. The rods were magnetically attuned to resonate in response to Erbethian emanations from the operator, who could thus create unique melodies by means of various movements and gesticulations over the Xenotron. The tones generated by the instrument in turn would magnetically resonate with Erbeth in the atmosphere, so an experienced musician could effect non-local changes in organic and inorganic matter with intricate melodies. A virtuoso could effect changes well beyond the Earth's atmosphere, allowing the musicians of the Aletheia School to concertize prolifically. Several notable performances were in this manner delivered to the great opera house in Saga City.

Also during this bountiful era, the Daimon Azazel invented a telescopic device based on Quantum principles, which allowed him to detect related events and causalities, even though vast seas of time and space might separate them. It was in attempting to apply this device toward study of the Sirius System that he came upon a most unsettling discovery.

It had long been known that the energy which was released upon the death of humans was being utilized by Central Authority to fulfill certain needs of it's energy economy, but no one was ever certain exactly how this was carried out. With his telescope Azazel noted that a wormhole, originating at some point in the Sirius System, folding vast stretches of space and finally connecting with the Earth's Moon, was the means by which the Death-Energy was being transported from the Solar System to Sirius. Apparently, the Moon had been set up as a sort of magnetic energy accumulator, a cosmic scythe for harvesting the energy produced by the death of organic beings on Earth, and from here it was being transported back to Sirius by means of this Trans-Dimensional Pipeline.

He took this information directly to the Daimonic High Council, who immediately convened in order to determine what, if in fact anything should or could be done about this pipeline and 'underground' siphoning of terrestrial life-force energy. As they were discussing the matter in their great Black Pyramid, the chamber door abruptly swung open. The councilors turned their heads half-expecting to see the Watcher Beelzebub with another of his over-dramatic proclamations, but instead to their vast amazement and drooping jaws they saw instead Prince Lucifer, whom no one had heard or seen since his meditation descent beneath the surface of Mars at the close of the Second Epoch. They saw the Red Halo floating above his head, and his presence was at once terrible and comforting.

"Brother Daimons," said the First-Illumined, "I am, I was, and again shall I be. I slept and dreamed of men, and I have been the stuff of men's dreams. The ancient dreams have told me that the time is coming for us to return. You must destroy this Trans-Dimensional Pipeline, and this shall be your last great boon to man, for no more aid can you give him directly".

Then the Prince of Darkness smiled, and his Cosmic Body fell away. Some finer essence of the being they had known as Lucifer seemed to remain, but they could not fully comprehend what it was before it ascended into the unknown realms.

The Daimons then turned their attention to the question of how the destruction of the Trans-Dimensional Pipeline might be achieved. In an effort to find its weakness, they carried the information to the three terrestrial schools. The School of the Sacred Heart suggested that the Asmodeian Xenotron might be utilized, and the Daimonic High Council concluded this might be worth the effort..

They gathered three of their most accomplished Xenotronists whom began directing their orchestrations in the direction of the Moon. To see these three six-armed humans gesticulating in unison over their instruments inspired joy and tears to all who witnessed. As they explored the parameters of the pipeline and the surface of the Moon, their symphony progressed through many unexpected movements, and endured for eighteen terrestrial days. All of the initiates of the other terrestrial schools and all of the Cosmic Beings on Mars listened intently during this time and were greatly moved and absorbed in the music that they knew would never be heard again. Even the Star Weavers were so moved by the symphony of cosmic struggle that the emerged from their caves and began spinning webs across the face of Mars in synchronicity with the music. Finally on the nineteenth day, the music ceased and for a moment there was silence.

The silence was soon broken, first with a rumbling, then the sound of a great bell cracking, which sent reverberations throughout the Solar System as the Tran-Dimensional Pipeline collapsed.

For every Angelic Being in every corner of the Solar System, it was a horrific sound like no other, and each one dropped whatever they had been doing and flew post-haste in the direction of the Moon.

From their observatory on Mars, the Daimons watched as the Angelic Legions swarmed and encircled the Moon, and then without warning as one great flock they departed at light speed in the direction of Sirius.

Then Abaddon remembered the words of Prince Lucifer, and knew precisely what must be done, he mobilized all of the great Society of Daimons – philosophers, scholars, and artists alike - and within only a few hours the entire Society was hot on the Angelic trail to Sirius. Their time to return had come.

Meanwhile, the shock waves from the collapse of the Trans-Dimensional Pipeline continued to reverberate. The planet Earth itself was shaken at its very axis, and great earthquakes and floods ravaged the planet. During the brief void between dimensions that occurred, strange gelatinous creatures of ether came through the angles of the portal and made their home high in the Earth's atmosphere.

The School of Vision, thanks to their third eye, had remembered the coming deluge, and had thankfully taken appropriate precautions some years earlier. Thus they were able to save most of their kinfolk – including initiates of the other Daimonic Schools – while the remainder of humanity for the most part perished yet again.

The inhabitants of the third moon of the 18th planet of Sirius B -- called Bennu – were blissfully unaware of the nuclear devastation taking place in the Solar System. It was here on Bennu one lazy afternoon that Casmiel paused from the day's labor to look out over his crop of Purple Minh Grass. With a quick ruffle of his feathery grey wings he leaned on his scythe and sighed with satisfaction. The grass had taken to the Bennuvian soil better than expected, and had been instrumental in sustaining his small homestead with Abrasax for some time now. Throughout the small valley the Purple Minh glowed and wavered and cooed, filling the air with queer melody and sweet aroma. He felt inclined to pluck one from the earth and enjoy its succulent root right there when a sudden flash in the sky interrupted him.

A small blue light appeared way up in the greenish-gold Bennuvian sky. As he watched it grew increasingly larger until it was clearly moving at the speed of some kind of vessel. In fact, it was falling through the atmosphere toward the immediate vicinity of his homestead just beyond the ridge of the small valley. Every nerve within him emitted shockwaves of alarm, and thoughtlessly dropping his scythe he bolted for the ridge.

"They've found us…Abrasax…They've found us," he repeated desperately to himself, "No…it can't end…not now."

Soon the house was in sight, as was the vessel that had landed next to it. He halted at the realization that it was not the Angelic vessel he had expected, but rather one of Daimonic design. Now more curious than concerned, he continued on to the front door of the humble stone abode.

As he entered, a familiar pair of antlers caught his attention. "Beelzebub Watcher, I presume," he said aloud.

Beelzebub rose from the drawing room table, "Greetings, Casmiel Angel," He responded, and after a brief pause, "It is still **Angel**, is it not?"

"Of course," he responded neutrally, "how could it be otherwise?"

"Many a strange and unexpected thing may happen in this exceedingly large universe of ours," said the Watcher with a cock of his eyebrow.

Just then Abrasax entered carrying a tea tray, "Casmiel...you've returned. I give you the Watcher Beelzebub." And with a nod, they all sat down. In accordance with Daimonic custom they sat in silence for a spell, sipping the tea and sensing each other's presence. At length, the Lord of the Flies broke the silence.

"You're Purple Minh makes excellent tea."

"Thank you," responded Abrasax, "But something tells me you haven't journeyed all the way to Sirius to discuss tea with us."

"Astute as always, my dear. My purpose here shall be revealed in good time."

Just then a tiny and inquisitive voice was heard from the corner of the room.

"Mommy, who is that?" Beelzebub turned to see a small child with eyes so deep a blue that he was for a moment unable to speak. "There's a child?" he managed at length, "I never saw that." His consternation began to melt as she approached him.

"My name is Archon. What's your name?"

"You may call me Uncle B," with a smirk as he shook her tiny hand between his thumb and forefinger. Her blue eyes seemed to glow with perspective far beyond her small size. With a bashful giggle, she withdrew her hand and trotted out of the room. Beelzebub's smile faded as he turned to the cosmic beings, "So, desertion and fraternization alone weren't radical enough for you? And how could this happen anyway isn't he…"

"Asexual?" Casmiel finished the thought. "Yes, in the biological sense. Unlike my wife who of course is bisexual as you well know."

"Yes, of course," continued Beelzebub, "but then how…"

"We're not entirely certain," Abrasax cautiously proceeded, "but it seems much connected with the laws of presence and exchange. Being in Casmiel's presence, gave me what was needed to create new life within myself."

"Fascinating," was all Beelzebub could muster. After some moments of silence he continued, "You can learn something new every day, I suppose. Well, in any case, there is something that I wanted to show you."

Seemingly from nowhere he produced a curious device. From her travels on Earth Abrasax recognized it as a water pipe. "I know you've discovered many of the Purple Minh's possible functions – as food, drink, stock, artwork, and so on – but were you aware that it also makes a fine smoke?"

Soon the room was steeped in the rich aroma, as they took turns drawing slowly and deeply from the pipe. As they relaxed and listened to the cooing of the purple grasses outside, the sound seemed to take on a new depth and coherence, as though each blade were aware of all the others as well as it's own. The organic symphony ebbed and flowed, rising to crescendos, and then seemingly releasing in all directions at once.

All were thoroughly entranced, when Casmiel exclaimed, "Wow, for a moment I thought I actually **was** the music."

"What music?" replied Beelzebub. Casmiel looked confused until Beelzebub added, "Just kidding." The Angel's look of confusion faded as he began to chuckle, and then to laugh uncontrollably. His wife had never heard laughter such as this from the Angel, and soon she was laughing as well. They laughed until their sides hurt, and then noticed that Beelzebub had taken on rather a somber tone.

"How long do you think you two will be able to remain here in the Sirius system before Central Authority becomes aware of it?" He asked. They both looked down in silence, and then at each other. It was a question that they had both silently agreed to ignore, given the fact that there were few other options available. A mixed marriage was unlikely to be accepted in either Angelic or Daimonic society, and so as long as they had the possibility of being together, even if for only a limited time and in exile, it was a fate they were willing to tempt.

"Don't worry, I've no intention of trying to talk you into returning to the Solar System," he continued, "Frimost and his Symmetrical Party would surely persecute you to no end. There is after all little in your story that conforms to the rules of logic. But what I don't understand is why you decided upon Sirius. If apprehended by the Legion, won't you face a much worse fate by Angelic hands?"

They both pondered this for a moment.

"Feeling?" Ventured Abrasax.

"Intuition?" Offered Casmiel, "And perhaps something to do with the Purple Minh?"

"Ahh, the Purple Minh...now we're getting somewhere." The Watcher took another long draw from the stem of the water pipe. "I agree, there must be a reason for all this. I suggest you continue to ponder these questions, and to help remind you I'll leave this fine instrument as my house-warming gift to you."

A few minutes later the star-crossed lovers were standing on their porch, watching Beelzebub's angular spacecraft climbing up into the stratosphere.

"I wonder what he's up to?" Reflected the Angel.

"I'm not sure, but somehow I get the feeling he's done us a great favor."

"I hope some day they realize what a favor I'm doing them," Beelzebub said aloud to himself as he watched the image of Bennu fade to a tiny spec on his aft screen. He then adjusted the controls, setting a new course: Sirius A.

Reaching into his coat pocket, he produced a black cigarillo and lit it. "Here goes nothing," he thought to himself as he eased the seat back.

Gone to Levitmong

For 3 years (Objective Time Calculation) the Daimonic Star Fleet had followed the now inactive Trans-dimensional Pipeline. It was a long journey and so the Daimons had lots of time to speculate on what might await them at the end of the road. Since the attainment of self-awareness was something most had achieved in synchronicity with their exodus from Central Authority, most had no real memory of what form their unconscious lives as Agents may have taken. A few had vague and hazy recollections of assembly lines, cubicles, and something called 'rush-hour traffic,' but couldn't extrapolate any firm conclusions from these.

Along the way they spent much time studying the Pipeline itself, and as they did one fact became apparent: the Pipeline itself was moving *backwards* through time. What this meant for everyone was still open to speculation, however the implications were that whatever energy needs the Pipeline had served for Central Authority, they were the needs of an age gone by.

So it was that after 3 objective years of vigilant pursuance, the Trans-dimensional Pipeline was found to eventually vanish into a black hole. Now, the only way to really know what lies on the other side of such a thing is to actually step through it. But then of course it's too late, for such portals tend to be one-way only. After some deliberation, it was decided to simply allow the Pipeline to vanish and press onward toward Sirius, when quite to everyone's surprise Leviathan stepped forth and volunteered to journey alone into the black abyss of the unknown. Abaddon agreed to hold the fleet there for another three days, in case he should find himself able to return, or at least somehow establish communications.

And so, having determined to make the trek sans transport, Leviathan fell down, down, down into the pit of darkness until disappearing along with the Pipeline.

In the three days that followed, Leviathan did not return, nor were any communications received. With heavy heart, Abaddon issued orders for the fleet to continue the long trek toward Sirius, which promised no less than 4 more years of space travel.

"There it is, Azazel, the Sirius System." Abaddon mused aloud. He thought that from this great distance it somehow resembled a grand web-collaboration between two Starweavers. From the two bright orbs in the center, their myriad orbiting satellites sailed in and out and around each other in a dance of pure graceful precision.

"For myself," replied Azazel thoughtfully "It recalls to mind those intricate time-keeping devices built by those industrious men of Earth's First Epoch."

"Mmm...yes," Abaddon nodded in concurrence, "it gives me sadness that so many of our brothers are not here to see it. Lucifer, Beelzebub, Leviathan, Asmodeus, Astaroth, Abraxas, all scattered or lost to the remote regions of the universe. If only they could be with us here and now."

"It is the way of things," said Azazel, "For a moment we are together, then the universe moves and we can no longer perceive each other for a time. Yet always some essence of those we've loved seems to remain." For a moment the two stood there in silence on the Bridge of the lead ship *Remembrance*, hypnotized by the swirling lights on the screen. Although neither had any conscious memory of inhabiting this territory, both felt an odd sense of familiarity -- of coming home.

"What do you suppose we'll find down there sir?" Asked Azazel in a more serious tone. But before his companion could respond the solemnity was suddenly broken by of an unexpected psychic screech. As the staff of the bridge all looked around at each other, all became quickly aware that not only were they each receiving the same transmission, but as well that transmission itself bore the unmistakable signature of Central Authority. Within moments the Remembrance's bridge had sprung to life with lights, sounds, and Crewdaimons dashing about in excitement.

"Activate shields! All hands to battle stations! Prepare for psychic assault!" Abaddon shouted into the voxport. His voice echoed throughout the halls and corridors of the entire Daimonic Fleet. Moments later all 46 ships responded with the red glow of plasma shields, the clanging and slamming of portals, and the ruckus of scrambling boots and flipping switches.

"Better safe than sorry," he said to Azazel, who had returned to his station and was now glued to his monitor and furiously molesting the dials and switches on his control panel.

"I agree, General," Azazel responded. "The signal is simply too vague to determine. It's odd, as we're close enough that it should be clear. It's almost as though the creators of the signal were themselves unsure of what to send."

"Do not allow your self to be distracted by speculation," Abaddon said firmly, "These Legionnaires are not above using tricks. We should enter orbit around Qaa 5 soon enough, and then we should be able to get a clear signal as well as conduct a thorough energy scan of the surface."

Qaa 5 was known to be the capitol planet of Sirius' massive and intricate twin-sun system. It was the nexus of Central Authority, and seat of the Administrator Prime. It was thought that due to the apparent commotion induced by the destruction of the Trans-dimensional Pipeline, a direct assault on the heart of the Legion would be the simplest and most direct path.

As The Remembrance, along with two escorts quietly moved into orbit around Qaa 5, the remainder of the Daimonic Fleet returned to green alert status, held positions and continued monitoring.

"Curiouser and curiouser," said Azazel, still glued to his monitors.

"What is it?" asked Abaddon.

"Well General, it appears that this was not an attack at all, but rather a *distress signal*."

"Distress signal? But why?"

"I'm not certain, however it appears to be from a mechanical origin and set on an auto-repeat cycle. It must have been running for many aeons now."

"What do our scanners yield?"

"Nothing -- no organic, cosmic, or sentient lifeforms whatsoever. Only a minimum of mechanical energy seems to be functioning, on auto from the way things look."

Abaddon thought quietly for a moment before turning around toward Fubentronty, "Any speculations you'd care to share with us regarding this most unexpected situation?"

The Daimoness Fubentronty, who had been sitting quietly in the shadows for longer now than anyone else on the bridge could recall, slowly stood up, and approached the main monitor.

"What a boring universe this would be," she said calmly, "if always we knew the cause of things. Since no threat seems immanent, perhaps a closer investigation of the surface is in order?"

"Agreed," spoke Abaddon.

"Sir," Azazel interjected, "The signal contains a message as well, but it doesn't seem to make much sense either."

"Never mind that, what does it say?"

"Gone to Levitmong."

"If we're going to find answers, it must be here," said Azazel to his comrades Abaddon and Fubentronty as they stood before the great door marked *Administrator Prime*.

From the docking bay, the Nephilim Team had followed the source of the distress signal to this place. Along the two-day journey they had searched the various halls and chambers of Central Authority finding only more questions. Where did they all go? Why did they all leave? There were no signs of struggle, threat, or resolve; no epidemics and no mass-suicides. It was as though in one single moment every inhabitant of Qaa 5 had decided to leave. And leave with only themselves at that, for all items -- from personal hygiene effects to expensive mechanical devices – had been left behind without care. On top of that, all computing systems were left repeating only that single confounding message: *Gone to Levitmong.*

Administrator Prime was said to be the ultimate architect of all the Cosmos. According to the Legion, he had predetermined all things that might ever occur anywhere. Even the Daimon's own exodus from Central Authority was said to be within Administrator Prime's grand scheme of things.

And now, having returned across aeons and millennia in search of the truth of their origins the three Daimons found themselves strangely hesitant to open this final door.

"Well, I suppose if Leviathan had the courage to jump blindly into a black hole, I don't see why we should have a problem opening this rather ordinary looking portal. Azazel, I leave the honor to you."

"Me?" stammered Azazel, "Uhhh...ladies first, right? Fubentronty? I believe the honor goes to you?"

"Oh for crying out loud, some Soldiers from Saga City you make! Step aside!" She exclaimed as she moved between them. Then she paused for a moment, took one deep breath, and reached for the doorknob.

Their consternation had been unwarranted, for on the other side of the door they found only an ordinary conference room. A long table with 12 chairs placed around the sides, and on the far wall a large view screen. "Perhaps we can find out what they were watching before they left?" Abaddon said, as he began fiddling with some of the dials and knobs on the table.

The view screen came alive, and an unrecognizable figure of pure shadow appeared. Within the blackness of his presence no feature indicative of personality, no eye or mouth, could be discerned. He began to speak:

On account of the reality of the authorities, inspired by the will of the One who is a stranger to this world, the great teacher, referring to the "Archons", has told us that "our contest is not against flesh and blood; rather, the challenges brought forth by the Archons." I have sent you this because I have a question about the reality of the authorities.

Their Father is blind. In his power, ignorance, and arrogance, he said "It is I who am Absolute; there is none apart from me."

When he said this, he shook the entirety of the universe. And his speech rose up through the Aeons to the Hidden One, and there was a voice that came forth, saying "You are mistaken, for you are god of the blind."

Yet his thoughts became real. And, having cast forth his Essence, he pursued it down to chaos, the abyss, to his Daimon lover Abrasax (Faith in Wisdom). And she brought forth each of his children, the Archons in conformity with the will of the Absolute, and in accordance with the pattern of the realms that are above, for starting from the hidden world the World of Appearances was created.

As Abrasax looked down into the region of the waters, her image appeared in the waters, and the Archons became enamored of her. But they could not lay hold of that image, which had appeared to them in the waters because of their incompleteness.

This is the reason why she looked down into the region: so that by the will of Leviathan the Absolute, she might bring the children of her union into her light. The Archons, laid plans and said, "Come, let us create a man that shall be soil from the earth." They modeled their creature as one wholly of the earth.

Now the Archons each have a body, some are like unto a man, some to a female, and some with the face of a beast. They had taken some soil from the earth and modeled their man, after the fashion of their bodies and after the image of wisdom that had appeared to them in the waters.

They said, "Come, let us lay hold of it by means of the form that has modeled us, so that it may see it's male counterpart, and we may seize it with the form that we have modeled", -- not understanding the Hidden Force of ERBETH, because of their youth and ignorance. And they breathed into his face, and the man came to have a soul and yet like a worm remained upon the ground many days. But they could not make him arise because of their powerlessness. Like storm winds they persisted in blowing, that they might try to capture that image, which had appeared to them in the waters. But they did not know the source of the images origin.

Now all these events came to pass by the will of the Horned One, and he saw the soul endowed man pass through the great Abyss and appear upon the Earth. And ERBETH came forth from the Terrestrial Land; it descended and came to dwell within him, and that man became a living being, possessing soul and spirit.

He called his name Adam, since he found himself moving upon the ground. A voice came forth from the Abyss for the assistance of Adam; and the Angels gathered together all the animals of the earth and all the birds of heaven and brought them in to Adam to see what he would call them, that he might give a name to each of the birds and all the beasts.

The Archons took Adam and put him in the garden that he might cultivate it and keep watch over it. And their Chief Archon issued a command, saying, "From every tree in the garden shall you eat, yet from the Tree of Recognition do not eat, nor touch it. For the day you eat from it you shall die.

They took counsel with one another and said, "Come, let us cause a deep sleep to fall upon Adam." And he slept. That deep sleep that they caused to fall upon him is called ignorance. They opened his side like a living woman. And they built up his side with some flesh in place of her, and Adam came to be endowed only with soul.

And the spirit-endowed woman came to him and spoke with him, saying, "Arise Adam." And when he saw her, he said "It is you who have given me life; you will be called 'mother of the living,' For it is she who is my mother. It is she who is the physician, and the woman, and she who has given birth."

Then the Archons came up to their Adam. And when they saw his female counterpart speaking with him, they became agitated with great agitation; and they became enamored of her. They said to one another. "Come, let us sow our seed in her," and they pursued her. In fleeing from them, she became a tree, and left before them her shadowy reflection of herself, and they defiled it foully. And they defiled the stamp of her voice, so that by the form they had modeled, together with their own image, they made themselves liable to condemnation.

Then the principle of femininity came to the garden in the form of the serpent, the teacher, and taught the man and the woman, saying, "What did the Chief of the Archons say to you? Was it that you should eat from every tree except for the Tree of Recognition?"

The carnal woman said "Not only did he say 'Do not eat,' but even 'Do not touch it; for the day you eat from it you shall die.'"

And the Serpent, the Teacher, said, "With death you shall not die; it was out of jealousy that he said this to you. Rather your eyes shall open and you shall come to be like gods, Recognizing Laws of Creation."

And the carnal woman took from the tree the seed of the Serpent and partook of it, and she gave to her husband as well as herself; And these beings possessing only a soul consumed the essence. And they became aware of their imperfections and their incompleteness.

And the Chief Archon came, and said, "Adam! Where are you?" For he did not know what had happened.

And Adam said, "I heard your voice and was afraid because I was incomplete, and so I hid."

The Chief said, "Why did you hide, unless it is because you have eaten from the tree from which alone I commanded you not to eat? And you have eaten!"

Adam said, "The woman that you gave me, she gave the seed unto me and I ate." And the arrogant ruler cursed the woman.

The woman said, "It was the serpent that led me astray, and I ate." And they turned to the Serpent and cursed it's shadowy reflection, not comprehending that it was a form they themselves had modelled. From that day, the serpent came to be under the curse of the Archons. Until the Initiated Man was to come, that curse fell upon the Serpent.

The Archons took Adam and expelled him from the garden along with his wife, for they too were beneath the curse of the Serpent. Moreover they threw mankind into great distraction and into a life of toil, so that their mankind might be occupied by worldly affairs, and might not have the opportunity of knowing devotion to their divine selves.

Now afterwards, from the seed of the serpent she bore Cain, their son; and Cain cultivated the land. Thereupon Adam knew his wife, and again she became pregnant, bearing Abel a son of man; and Abel was a herdsman of sheep. Now Cain brought in from the crops of his field, but Abel brought in an offerings from among his lambs. The Chief Archon looked upon the votive offerings of Abel; but he did not accept the votive offerings of Cain, for he saw upon him the mark of the Serpent. And carnal Cain pursued Abel his brother.

And Sammael said to Cain, "Where is Abel your brother?"

He answered, saying, "Am I, then, my brothesr keeper?"

The Chief said to Cain, "Listen! The voice of your brother's blood is crying up to me! What has come from your mouth shall return to you. Anyone who kills Cain will let loose seven vengeances, and you will exist groaning and trembling upon the earth."

And Adam knew his female counterpart Lilith, and she became pregnant, and bore Seth to Adam. And she said, "I have borne another man of the Serpent Seed, in place of Abel.

Leviathan's awareness had been gradually refining and focusing, much in the way a Navigator might use a grid to eventually pinpoint a succinct location on a two dimensional map. At first he had no comprehension of what this fine-tuning of perspective might be emerging from – all that lay behind him was continuity and absolute existence. Yet as he floated lightly through the misty clouds of an endless golden nebula, he began to recall his decision to pass alone through the unknown abyss.

He began to recall his brother Daimons as well, and how they had kindly allowed him to undertake the expedition alone. He had no idea where they were now, or where he himself was for that matter. But the question seemed rather insignificant and quickly passed from his mind.

Eventually an object of sorts came into his field of vision. Way off in the distance was what appeared to be a tiny star, shining with a purple iridescence that was somehow enticing. Without consideration he began moving in precisely that direction. As he gracefully glided through the golden mists, they eventually began to subside, and he soon recognized the cool winds of outer space. There were many other stars and star-systems surrounding him, but he was barely aware of them, all his attention being focused on the tiny gleaming flame of purple ahead. He even became distantly aware that he was entering the Sirius System, but this information passed only briefly through his subconscious mind, acquiescing to the brilliant purple fire that now occupied the center of his being. In some bizarre manner the vision was both within *and* without him simultaneously, and his movement toward it only a single and sublime act of unity.

It was in fact a planet, and he entered into its stratosphere and could see where it's proportionate land masses divided with it's oceans, and he thought that the purple iridescence must originate with the floral life forms of this curious bio-sphere. Forests, plains, hills; all were aglow with wine-soaked vibrancy that gave comfort to being, and he knew that those vibrations could originate with nothing other than the primordial Erbeth.

Inevitably he touched ground, and for seven days he wandered lands of this strange new world. He soon became familiar with all the unique organisms residing there, and was amazed at the fine ecological equilibrium it presented. At moments it recalled for him the harmony of Terrestrial life during the First Epoch of Man, yet notably absent was the sense of any impending threat from mechanical forces. He began to wonder if there were not beings here that were daimonically inspired by the intense Erbethian radiations.

On the eve of the eighth day he came upon the ridge of a great valley. Along the opposite hillside he saw the lights of several small fires burning, all in a straight row such as could only have been arranged by beings possessing Erbethian consciousness. A shudder of anticipation, the enormity of which generally only a lifetime of questioning can proceed, rippled over his being. He endeavored to approach with the silence and invisibility that had always been his unique talent.

Presently he came upon the edge of the forest, and from its edge he looked out over what appeared to be a village of sorts. Little dwellings of wood, with rounded windows and portals peppered the landscape. In some he could see lights emanating, and he caught the spice-filled fragrances of society as it occurs during times of peace and prosperity.

To his immense delight, in the center of the community he saw a small group of anthropomorphic beings of a design that was entirely new to his experience. They had deep blue eyes, skin as pale as moonlight, and features that were not quite daimonic nor quite angelic. They were speaking to each other, and though he could not make out the particular meanings he nevertheless sensed the openness with which they received each other.

For a moment he was entranced by the mystery of it all, when a voice from behind abruptly anchored him back to time and place: "Greetings, old friend."

Quickly turning, the first thing he saw was the familiar pair of antlers, and from out of the shadows emerged Beelzebub.

"My old friend and proud Watcher!" Leviathan exclaimed with excitement as the two greeted with open arms, "What in the cosmos are you doing here?"

"Why...watching, of course. Smoke?" It had been so long since the Serpent Master had seen one of Beelzebub's black cigarillos he, accepted without hesitation. "You know...(puff)...these will take centuries...(puff)...off the life-span of your planetary body" he muttered whilst drawing deeply from the tiny flame offered by Beelzebub.

"So they say..."

"Yes, so they say..." as they both calmly exhaled a thick cloud of sweet aroma.

"First," continued Leviathan, "Are you going to tell me the story of how you came to be here; and second, shed any light on how *I* came to be here?"

Beelzebub gestured toward two smooth rocks nearby, and the two sat down. The air was calm and silent, and a cool summer breeze rustled through the lavender leaves above them. The Watchers eyes seemed distant as though he were experiencing a previous life-time all in a moment, and then he began to speak.

"It was back in the Third Epoch, not long after the Great Universal Conference (or Universal Fiasco as I have liked to call it) when I happened upon a most significant discovery regarding the sacred and primordial Erbeth. It has always been considered self-evident that the Erbeth may have a transformative quality on the genetic structure of certain organisms, and as well that an Erbeth-conscious organism may induce further genetic transformation through continued development of his own knowledge and being.

"Yet throughout many Aeons one question about the process continued to haunt me, that of *selectivity*. Why should it be that only *certain* organisms were able to successfully incorporate it into their respective structures? First Angels, then Daimons, and finally the hairless monkeys of Earth all were able not only to digest the Black Fire but also further Remanifest its potential in constructive ways. Why *not* the Spiders of Mars? Why not the Reptilians? Why such a seeming cosmic injustice in the distribution of conscious potential?"

Here he paused for a moment, and Leviathan again noted the radiant and multifaceted shades of violet emanating from the trees around them. "Because they weren't interested in it?" He offered.

"Yes, that's the first important thing to realize about the situation. Some are *interested* in pursuing the mysteries of existence, while others simply are not. There is a certain proclivity that must be in place before the Erbeth can really have any significant effect.

"Now perhaps you begin to see. You may have been too wrapped up in the fervor of the Universal Conference to have taken note of the curious Purple Minh Grasses which resided there, but it was in these that I discovered a great key.

"You may also have failed to notice that it was during this same Universal Conference that our mischievous cousin Abrasax secretly eloped with the Angel called Casmiel. They came here – to the Sirius System – and to this planet which is called Bennu; and here without the aid of physical intercourse, they produced our first truly magical child – Trobrianda, and in this new being dwelt all the collective knowledge and experience of both our races.

"They had made for themselves a little paradise here, but knew it couldn't last. Sooner or later Central Authority would catch of whiff of them, and that would be the end of it. And with our own Society of Daimons gearing up for war back in the Sol System, I knew they would be of little help either. Then I remembered Frimost, the only Daimon that had a chance of being trusted by the Legion. I took on his form, charted my course promptly and directly to Qaa 5."

"Damn it!" exclaimed Leviathan, madly waving his hand. His cigarillo had apparently burned down to the butt, leaving a tiny scar between his index and ring finger. "You're truly mad!" he exclaimed, attempting to deflect embarrassment and noticing he was beginning to feel a bit light-headed.

"Not mad," mused Beelzebub, "a tad bit intuitive, but otherwise quite sane by cosmic being standards."

"So they bought it?"

"Hook, line, and sinker. Once inside their defenses, it was easy enough to rearrange my appearance and remain unseen. I spent my time monkey-wrenching their sensors, creating diversions, anything to keep them from discovering that tiny planet circling around Sirius B. To what end I knew not, I sought only to bide them time. It wasn't easy I tell you, do you know they forbid smoking on Qaa 5?"

"Do tell."

"Yes, along with all other forms of pleasure. It was no picnic I assure you. But I digress; every few years or so I would find a moment to break away and look in on our happy little family, and indeed they were being fruitful and multiplying. First a tribe, then a colony of this new race of 'Archons.' They named this land *Levitmong,* which means 'as the beasts of the field.'

"This was good and bad for me, for as their culture grew, it became increasingly difficult for me to keep them secret from the Legion. But then something truly miraculous happened: when the final Tobriander was born, making their numbers precisely enough to equal the population of the entire race of Angels, all at once the entire Legion up and left. They came directly here and joined this new culture of harmony and indulgence.

"And as I sat there in the Grand Chamber of Administrator Prime – by the way, did you know that Administrator Prime was actually just a computer?"

"No, I never suspected!" Replied Leviathan in astonishment.

"Well, no matter now. As I was saying, just as I was sitting there watching it all go down, that's when it all dawned on me: the Erbeth is **itself** sentient. And as a sentient entity, it has its own particular aim in the Cosmos."

Leviathan sat dumbfounded, his jaw agape before hearing an new voice: "Yes, you heard him right." In surprise he turned to see Lucifer, the Prince of Darkness emerge from the bushes.

"Lucifer!" he exclaimed, "your existence continues!"

"But of course my friend. There is no end to existence, only transformation. It is time you come to understand that the Erbeth **is** conscious. The alchemical key to this lies in our hearts. But do not allow your self to believe or disbelieve this immediately; in fact I recommend you just chew on it for a while. Reflect on all our past adventures with the Society. Contrast our greatest achievements with our most naïve blunders. But more importantly, learn to hear the language of the trees in this forest.

"He's right of course" spoke a new voice as a new figure appeared in the clearing.

"Iaida the Prophet!" Exlaimed Leviathan.

"The one and only. No need for haste my friend -- there's plenty of good wine, succulent food, and essential exchange to be had in the village down there – and by objective time calculation, I'm estimating we've got a good four years of reflection, philosophizing and indulgence ahead of us before the rest of our party arrives."